THE PRESIDENT

THE PRESIDENT

Xander Beattie

PRONK

FOR
BRETT MURRAY
AND
IN MEMORY OF
DULCIE SEPTEMBER
AND
MY BELOVED
RHODA KADALIE

Prologue

Is this how the story ends?

On a roof. Adam is watching the crowd in the square below, the liquid jostling, fists spiking the air, chants rippling up to him. An armoured vehicle has been swallowed by the sea.

He crouches, eyes closing. Forces them open again, peers down. The pangas' glinting pricks his eyeballs. He sees a man in a red beret with a megaphone yelling, his fist raised. No one is looking up; no one has spotted him – yet.

One storey below, Zandile is opening the French windows, walking out onto the balcony. Now the marchers are looking up, yelling, this crowd, no meaning received in the unanswerable roar. She's yelling back but he can't tell what she's saying, there are no words under the sun today, no words, only voices, one voice shouting. A glass bottle shatters against the wall behind her.

'Zandile!' he screams.

Adam is flying to the trapdoor; his legs are melting down the steps into the office's gloom. A meteor swims across a screen, a new email pings, the outside presses in through the windows gently, like distant breakers.

The front door surrenders. The crowd gushes in and upwards. Zandile sinks down, holding her knees and shutting her eyes.

They can smell blood. They are in the building – how many of them? Adam and Zandile both know this. He's pulling her up and she is awake and blinking. Her hand is sticky, her arm is coated in streaks of blood.

'Come' – maybe he's saying. Or maybe he is just holding the stickiness and pulling her into the passage and maybe they are on the staircase now.

Adam looks down at the heads: there are beanies and berets and a flatcap floating up towards them. He slams the door to the office shut.

'There,' Adam says, pointing at the fire door. He yanks this open and they are outside next to an air conditioner unit and the drainpipes, staring down at the rubbish bins and the poetry of paint splattered on concrete.

Zandile is livelier now; she can keep up with Adam, almost, as they glide down, down. Then the metal steps stop, metres above the ground, and Adam's jumping down and yelling 'Fuck!' His knees greet the ground. His body crumples, legs shaking. He gets up, arms outstretched, embracing Zandile as she slips off the last step.

They topple together, down, down, until their heads bounce against the concrete. Up. He pulls her up. She sways like she's falling asleep; he almost slaps her – they need to move!

SUNDAY

[1]

Max feels better when it is finished. Something has at least softened: the unintelligible became words and the words escaped onto the paper in stern, defiant scribbles. He closes the notebook. It's not very good; he will read it tomorrow and see that. But it is something, and it has made him feel better, and that, surely, is a small victory to be celebrated. Especially – unlike the other stories, this one he will liberate from the notebook; he will type it up tomorrow; he will send it to that online journal whose founders he heard being interviewed on the radio this afternoon.

He smiles. *Vula*. Open. He tries to imagine what they look like, Adam and Zandile. Their voices had sounded young, perhaps not that much older than he is. Are they lovers? He wants to Google them, he wants to visit *Vula*'s website, too, but he will rather wait until he has a chance to use one of the computers in the public library; that way is safer. He will go tomorrow.

TUESDAY

[2]

'This was in the letter box,' says Zandile as she comes into the office. She hands Adam a manila envelope with his name scribbled on the front. Adam tears open the side; when he tugs out the slip of paper from inside, a small flash stick falls out onto the desk. He reads the handwritten note.

Dear Adam

On the accompanying flash stick is a story
I've written that I would like to submit to "Vula".
Please pardon its unconventional delivery,
but I don't feel comfortable using email.

Sincerely,
Gabriel Roberts

He shows Zandile the note. 'Do you think this is a joke?'
'Only one way of finding out.'
He grunts, leans forward to insert the flash stick into the side of his computer. He opens the only file, a document titled "The President".
'Take a look,' he tells Zandile after he's finished reading it. He won't say anymore than that for now. He has a slight hard-on. He picks up a notebook, shields his groin with it as he stands up. He goes to the row of sash windows with his coffee as she sits down. It's raining. Below, people are dashing across the square; taillights dribble past, but he can't hear the cars.
Zandile reads slowly. She turns to him.
'Sheesh, Adam. I like it. What do you think?'
He shrugs. 'It's a bit porno.'
'It's graphic, but does that matter? It's saying something important.'
'What's it saying, then?'
'That appearances can be deceiving. Don't take everything at face value.'
'A secretly queer president being fucked by a rent boy. That is what it's

saying. I'm not convinced of the literary merit of that.'

'Oh come on! It's evocative, imaginative, asking readers to look beyond the certainties of heteronormative patriarchy. It's saying, don't assume! And I like how it depicts the president as bit of a monster, but also so vulnerable and so human – a victim, in a way, of his culture and upbringing.'

'Most of it's an extended sex scene.'

'So what? Since when did you become such a prude?'

Adam sighs. 'Anyway, who is this Gabriel Roberts? We don't have a clue. Don't you think it's weird he didn't email it to us? A flash drive in the letter box; that's a tad cloak-and-dagger, no?'

'You're trying to come up with excuses. Stop being a wuss. We should totally publish this. Now, I've got to get some work done.'

Time does help, yes. As the minutes, hours, days accumulate, the roar lowers to an insistent hush. But now, returning here six weeks later, it is back and loud – a scream. Max reads a battered *GQ*, and it is the same one he was reading – or trying to read – when he was waiting for Dr Khumalo last time. Of course in those minutes before meeting with her, there was just the pain and the fear: he didn't know yet, before the prescription pad came out, about the pills – just how many there would be: three different antiretrovirals, two once a day, one twice a day for a month; the week of nausea and vomiting and runny shits they gave him. The chlamydia pill – taken twice a day during the first week. And the five pills for trichomoniasis he swallowed in one go, unleashing a series of violent cramps.

Dr Khumalo hadn't completely believed his story – that was obvious. Not that he was lying; he was offering her a neatly packaged version, scrubbed of context, that he had repeated in his head on the walk to the medical practice: a guy he didn't know well had fucked him without a condom.

'Max.'

He looks up. Dr Khumalo is at her door, smiling.

Inside her room, she asks him how he is feeling. 'A lot better. Like you said, the initial stage was horrible – the nausea mostly.'

She nods. 'And. Are you sure you don't want to talk about this? About whatever happened? It doesn't have to be to me – I could refer you to a psychologist.'

He shakes his head. 'I'm fine.'

She raises an eyebrow, but does not push him.

'Now that you're out of the window period, we're going to do the rapid

HIV test and get the results for that now. And then we'll take your bloods and get a urine sample done to confirm you're in the clear for everything else. I can email those results to you when I get them back from the lab on Wednesday.'

He doesn't need to know if the pills he took worked their precautionary magic. It doesn't matter. He's tempted to tell her that, to say – Don't bother, leave them in a file. But his indifference would only trigger more questions, wouldn't it? Why had he even bothered to go to her six weeks ago? He was flailing, it was something to do; he'd wanted reassurance, maybe, something to hold on to, something he could do about what had happened.

When she shows him the one line – negative for HIV – he feels a welling deep in his chest. Is he reacting to the result, or to the reminder of what brought him here, of why he's getting tested? He tries, at first, to tamp it down, but the insistent, incomprehensible flood is surging up anyway. So what. For now, in this consulting room, with this kind-eyed doctor, he is safe. Through his sobbing he sees her get up from her chair and come towards him. She takes his hand and squeezes it tightly.

Susannah glares at Max when he enters the bookshop a few minutes late for his shift. He mumbles an apology as he shrugs out of his dripping raincoat.

'Don't get the books wet,' she hisses.

He doesn't answer; instead, he walks to the rear, through the open door into the tiny kitchen. Hangs his coat up on the hook.

Later, when he is packing away a new batch of battered Agatha Christies, a middle-aged man brushes past him. Max stiffens as the bulk of him sidles past. He scrunches his eyes tight, leans closer to the shelves. The man has already ventured to the corner; he is metres away when Max opens his eyes, but still, he feels the press of him, the insinuating, soft press of him. He puts the books down. He walks to the back, down the three steps to the toilet.

He doesn't vomit; he just stands, waits for the feeling to pass. He breathes in deeply. When he goes back into the shop, the man is still there, reading. His grey hair is short; he has a neat goatee. Light from naked bulbs overhead flash against his spectacles. He didn't do it on purpose, Max tells himself – he was just walking past.

He will try to think about other things. About the story. But that is a worry, too. He is not convinced dropping off the flash drive today was the right way of doing it. What if it doesn't reach this Adam guy? What if they don't check their letter box – after all, who gets mail these days?

There is a cough.

'Edmund White,' says a wispy voice.

Max turns. The man is right next to him. 'Do you have any Edmund White? You know. The gay writer?'

He shakes his head. 'No. No Edmund White. Sorry. We sold our last copy of *A Boy's Own Story* about a week ago.'

The man nods. Max turns back to the shelf, continues slotting newly arrived paperbacks into their correct spots. He hears the bookshop's door open; only once it shuts do his shoulders loosen.

WEDNESDAY

[3]

Once the small talk is out of the way, Adam gives the printed sheets to Ms Thomson. They have already ordered – they will share a pot of Earl Grey like they always do. While she reads, he glances around the hotel verandah. Ferns in porcelain pots dwarf either side of their sofa. The grand piano has struck up in the lounge – "A Nightingale Sang in Berkeley Square" wafts through the open door. A waitress crosses the chequered floor, stoops down to their table with a tray; Adam thanks her.

Ms Thomson doesn't look up. He inspects her while she reads. She's no different, really, to what she was like at school: still the slash of red lipstick and a pageboy cut – although, nine years later, grey strands interrupt the black.

She puts the pages down, a small smile gleaming as she pours tea into both their cups.

'It's not exactly subtle,' she purrs.

Adam nods.

'Why not publish it? I sometimes feel like the fire has gone out of the belly of local literature. We burn down libraries instead of housing inflammatory writing in them.'

Adam smiles. 'So, you think we should go ahead?'

Ms Thomson nods. 'Remember your final creative writing exam. You used the word 'cunt'. You didn't really need to. The story could have stood without it. But I knew that letting you use it gave you something much more important – it gave you the confidence and the freedom to write uncensored. If you publish this you're sending a message – you're saying to young writers: 'You can write what you like.' And surely that's what this country needs?'

'You make it sound so noble.'

Ms Thomson sips from her teacup.

'Perhaps, darling, it is.'

FRIDAY

[4]

Max disembarks at Salt River, two stops short of Cape Town Station. Seagulls swoop and scatter over the rails as the train slithers on towards town. He sits down on a bright blue bench, takes out a paperback. When the next train sidles up to the platform less than 20 minutes later, he's still on the same page of *Middlemarch* (though he has figured out the locations of the station's CCTV cameras – or at least the four of them in plain view). He notices a man hobble into the carriage through the doors at its other end. A man with a cane and sunglasses – blind? Or is that just an act?

The train judders along to Woodstock. The man with the cane has sat down, staring straight ahead. Max wants to get off, wants to run, but he stays put as the train continues.

At Cape Town Station, he is the first to exit the carriage. He does not look back. Instead, he jogs through the ticket barrier onto the concourse. In its centre, he freezes. Neck swiveling, looks around. Five CCTV cameras, no, six. No wonder he can't shake off the feeling he's being watched. He strides to the Strand Street exit, exhaling as his feet step onto the pavement. He dashes across the intersection, in defiance of the glowing little red man. The minibus taxi which nearly smashed into him is hooting furiously. No other pedestrians have been reckless enough to follow him over; two are standing, waiting for the light to change (neither of them are the supposedly blind man, thank God). His run has mellowed to a jog but he is scared of going any slower. If he did have a tail, surely by now he's shaken it off? Regardless, that being-watched feeling is stubbornly sticking around. And so, he won't dawdle – just in case.

The doorbell chimes.

'It's your turn to get it,' Zandile says.

Adam stretches his arms wide, yawns. 'Fine.'

He goes to the handset screwed into the wall.

'Hello?'

The voice is soft and deep: 'Um, hi, it's um, Gabriel Roberts here.'

'Oh, the guy who wrote the story?'

'Yes. I was wondering… I just wanted to check if you got it…'

'Yep, we got it.'

'Cool. OK then…'

'Why don't you come up?' Adam says suddenly. 'We'd love to meet you.'

There is a pause. 'I really don't think…'

Adam is too curious to not insist. 'Come on, man.'

Silence.

'I'm opening the door.'

Adam presses the buzzer, hoping he hasn't scared him off. He turns to Zandile. 'Guess who's here? Gabriel Roberts!'

Zandile is grinning smugly.

'What?'

She shakes her head. 'Nothing. Nothing at all.'

He jogs down the three flights of stairs to the narrow entryway. Waiting behind the locked security gate is a guy wearing a grey beanie and skinny jeans, his hands hidden in the pockets of his bomber jacket.

'Hi there,' Adam says, fumbling with the key. Finally it turns; the gate opens.

Gabriel steps hesitantly forward, pushing his spectacles up his nose.

'Hi, I'm – '

'Gabriel, right?'

He coughs. 'I'm Max, actually. Gabriel's a pseudonym. Sorry.'

'I'm Adam.'

They shake hands.

'Come on up.'

Max follows Adam's *veldskoen* up the gloomy steps. They reach the second storey, enter a bright room.

A Black girl in her late twenties – about the same age as Adam, Max suspects – is sitting at one of two iMacs, her back straighter than a yogi's. On the exposed brick walls are framed prints of book covers (Orwell's *1984* and *Why I Write*; Steve Biko's *I Write What I Like*). A bookshelf is crammed with books.

'Zandile, this is Gabriel Roberts, aka Max…'

Zandile gets up. The floorboards creak as she walks over to them. She shakes his hand.

'I thought you were going to be a dirty old white guy,' she chuckles. 'It's nice to meet you. Max.'

Max grins. 'Likewise.'

'How old are you exactly?'

'25.'

'Ah. Older than you look. And what do you do?'

'I'm doing my master's. English literature. At UCT.'

She nods.

Max looks at the windows praying he won't be asked any other questions, that he won't be reckless enough to answer them.

'OK, enough interrogating,' Adam says. 'Fancy a coffee, Max?'

'A coffee! Ad, it's almost five on a Friday,' Zandile says. 'Check if there's beers in the fridge. Or wine. It's a red wine kind of day, isn't it?"

Max knows: he should go now. He must not drink. This was a mistake. He should not have come to their office.

Adam disappears to the kitchen.

'I liked your story, Max,' Zandile says.

'Thanks.'

'What was the inspiration behind it?'

He stares down at the gleaming wooden floorboards. He looks up at her. 'I don't know. It just kind of came to me.'

She nods. He can see she's sceptical.

Adam returns with three wine glasses in one hand, an opened bottle of red wine in the other. He sets everything down on a trestle table, pours the wine.

'Cheers,' he says, handing glasses to Zandile and Max.

Max raises his glass.

'So we might as well tell you – I don't know if Zandile has already,' Adam says. 'We're going to run your story. Thanks for sending it to us.'

Max gulps. 'Thank you.' He should go. What's he doing here? He doesn't know what else to say. He takes another sip of wine, an even bigger one.

'Nice wine.'

'It's one of our clients. We do their branding.'

He nods.

'Max, you're not from this country, are you?' asks Zandile.

'No, I am.'

'But your accent's a bit... English or something.'

'I lived in London when I was young.'

Zandile nods. 'What do you parents do?'

'Shame, stop giving the guy the third degree,' interjects Adam.

'No, it's OK,' Max says. Lie, lie, lie. He is tempted to say nothing more.

But then he offers, 'My dad's in business. My mom passed away.'

'I'm sorry,' Zandile says.

'It was long ago. I was an infant.' He refrains from telling them more. That it was a letter bomb delivered to her at the university in Maputo. That the blast had killed his mom and her research assistant instantaneously. That, sleeping in a carry-cot under a desk, he'd been spared. He looks at Zandile who – annoyingly – still wears a pitying look. Asks, 'How did you two meet?'

'College. First year. We've been pretty much inseparable ever since,' replies Zandile.

He nods. They're together, then. Oh well. He glances at Adam, who's looking at him. He looks quickly away.

'Now, I hate to be a party-pooper, but I've got to be getting back to Bjorn – he's been in bed with flu the whole day,' Zandile says. She takes one more sip, sets down the half-empty glass. She turns to Max. 'It was lovely meeting you. You should totally pop by the office again. Ad, don't forget to lock up properly.'

She kisses Adam on the cheek.

'Bye-bye, darlings,' she says at the door. They listen to the clatter of her shoes on the stairs, steadily softening.

'Who's Bjorn?'

'Her fiancé.'

'Fiancé? But – you?'

Adam giggles. 'No way, dude.'

Max looks down into his glass. 'Sorry.'

'Don't apologise. People assume that all the time.'

Adam reaches for the bottle, pours more into their glasses. He stands up and sinks down onto the couch next to Max where Zandile had been sitting.

'Are you enjoying varsity?'

Max nods. 'Harvard referencing aside, I absolutely love it.'

'I sometimes wished I'd studied literature. But I was shit scared I wouldn't get a job, and I wanted to do something creative so I thought copywriting would be the next best thing.'

'You didn't study literature?'

'And yet I have the temerity to edit a literary journal, I know. Outrageous!'

'Sorry, I didn't mean it like that. I just thought...'

Adam shrugs. 'Hopefully my enthusiasm and excellent taste make up for my lack of academic cred. Of course there are times I feel hopelessly out of my depth. But that's all part of the fun. Learning on the job.' He gets up, goes to the window. 'Fuck, it's raining again. I was going to cycle home. I've got an idea, though. Do you fancy another drink, and maybe a bite to eat?'

'I really ought to be getting home,' Max says.

'You sure?'

Max looks up at him. The light is making Adam's hair glow: the neat blonde strands look so soft. He is being ridiculous. He should go. He *must* go. He shivers, looking away. Is he drunk?

'Fine, guess I better eat something,' he hears himself saying. He stands up slowly. 'Can you tell me where the bathroom is?'

Adam explains. Max gets up, walks slowly. He breathes in. He reaches the staircase, goes down one flight, opens the door to the bathroom. Puts the light on. Stares at himself. He looks wan, sickly almost, in the fluorescent's glare. He takes off his specs, rubs his eyes. Takes off his beanie, stuffs it into his pocket. Pulls off the band that sheathes the short dreads sprouting from his crown. Both hands swipe them backwards, converge. He squeezes the tips, twists the band on again. A bit better. But what is he doing? He stares at his eyes. This is dangerous. He should go. But it is dark, and raining.

'Stop it,' he whispers to himself. 'For once, just fucking stop it.'

He turns the tap. Washes his hands with the small, cracked cake of soap, cups his hands and bends down to splash his face.

It will be fine. He takes a deep breath and tells himself that. It will be absolutely fine.

The Power and the Glory's interior is thick with smoke and chatter and The Black Keys. A cigarette, in mid-gesticulation, narrowly misses Adam's eye as he sidles between drinkers towards the gents. He spots Sophy, an old friend of Raees's, at the end of a long table. Thankfully she's not looking in his direction – awkward encounter averted. In front of the urinal, he pulls out his phone. Zandile has messaged: Are you boys having sex yet?

Adam replies: Lol. No. Just drinking.

As he pisses, his phone vibrates in his pocket. Come on. Make a move. He's a cutie.

He washes his hands. He's tempted to explain to Zandile – he's not ready. And Max isn't even interested, probably. The screen waits. Finally, he types: I know.

He goes to the bar. He needs fortifying. Or loosening up. Both, really. He has to wait while others are served. He's squeezed up against an ancient leather jacket, wet; it smells like dog. "Lonely Boy" has come on again. He taps his foot in approval, leans forward to ask the pigtailed woman pouring draft beer if he can get two double whiskies with ice.

Finally he is free of the crush; he steps down into the quieter café area where people are sitting with their beers and wine, hot dogs and brownies. Max has taken off his beanie again. He's reading something; totally still, absorbed. He must have forgotten about his Sauvignon Blanc – there's still a gulp or two left.

As Adam puts the whiskies down, he looks up.

'Sorry, should've checked if you drank whisky. I'll have this if you don't.'

'I do. Sometimes,' Max says, closing his book.

'Good old Zadie, eh. I really enjoyed *On Beauty*. But then I am an E. M. Forster fan. Did you know it was inspired by *Howards End*?'

Max nods.

'We haven't really chatted about your story.'

Max shrugs, takes a sip of the whisky. 'Do you ever write?'

'Other than copy, you mean? Hardly ever. It's too hard. I love reading, though. Zandile does too. I guess that was one of the reasons we started *Vula*.'

'What are the others?'

'Just after finishing high school, I was on holiday with my dad and my stepmom. And I met this cute guy about my age and we made out and he gave me a hand job in the hotel toilet. It was my first intimate encounter and I felt totally overwhelmed. I hadn't told my dad I was gay yet and this secret was suffocating me and the only way I could deal with everything was to write it out, turn it into a story. I used a pseudonym and I sent it to *Horizon* – which is the oldest literary journal in the country, I think. The editor's like 80 and they only print 300 copies or so but you get serious kudos if it publishes your work.'

'Yes, I've heard of *Horizon*.'

"Well, they took about six months to respond – I had already forgotten about the story, in fact I think I had come out to my parents by then. And you know what they said, what the editor told me? We like your style – it's vivid, elegant, blah blah, but frankly, your story is rather risqué, and that masturbation bit is far too graphic. Would you care to tone it down and resubmit?

'And I was like fuck you, and didn't even bother to reply. Ever since then I wanted to start my own magazine, where people could write about stuff, real stuff, and where they wouldn't be censored like that.'

Adam holds his glass up, stares into the amber liquid. He's a fucking hypocrite, isn't he? He remembers his whining to Zandile – he had accused Max's story of being 'porno', of lacking literary merit. Was he any different to the old codger at the helm of *Horizon*?

'*Vula*'s awesome,' Max says. 'I'm really pleased you're publishing my story.'

Adam smiles; it's the first time he's seen him animated like this. 'What inspired it? I mean, what made you write about, well, a gay president?'

Max's smile fades. 'Does it matter?'

He shrugs, unwilling though, to let this go. 'Do you know people in politics?'

Max cocks his head to one side, then turns to look at the window. 'If I did,' he finally murmurs, 'do you really think I would write something like that?'

The clouds have gone; the city has reappeared, sparkling silently below him. Max shoves the French doors open wider, leans over the railing, lights a cigarette.

He has not asked Adam for permission to smoke, but he is too alert, he needs it to calm down, and he doesn't want to wake him. Water pipes groan somewhere in the building. A cat is patrolling between the parked cars two storeys below; it stops to lick at a shiny puddle. Is he still drunk? He definitely was when they left the bar at 12; the glow of his watch's hands suggests it's just after three now. Ash is flicked. Another draw. He leans forward again, exhaling smoke into the night.

When they'd finished the whiskies, Adam suggested they call it a night. Max unspools the fading sequence now – watches them weave between the tables covered in wine stains and candlewax drippings. Outside they waited for a moment, watching the drizzle, the taxis leaping up the hill. They followed the bar's perimeter, looking in on the candles, the huddling. In the locked-up entrance of the bottle store, Adam tugged him closer. Max knew he could run, but he didn't. He felt Adam's lips touch his. Gently. He opened his eyes. 'Let's go,' said Adam, and he followed him. The walk up the hill, turning into a side street, is blurry, sharpening to the moment in the hallway, under the light when they kissed again. Their wet soles made milky prints on the parquet. Adam pulled off Max's jacket. Max unbuttoned Adam's check shirt, his corduroys. In the bedroom they stood watching each other – wordless, naked. A bedside lamp threw their shadows against the white wall. Adam almost stepped forward to touch him but stopped; his hand fell to the side. A draft brushed past them from the slightly-opened window. Max shivered. 'Can I get in?' he asked, and Adam, impassively, nodded. In bed they lay together, both facing up. Max yawned and turned away, onto his side; he could feel Adam leaning into him. He froze as Adam's hand tentatively touched his dick. The hand fell away, and he relaxed. He liked this warmth, the skin and hair against his back. They must have fallen asleep simultaneously.

Max wants to smoke another cigarette but he doesn't. He wants to leave this flat but he doesn't. Instead, he walks back to the bedroom, and climbs back into bed.

SATURDAY

[5]

Instead of sex – pancakes.

Adam pulls the eggs and milk out of the fridge, a pan from the cupboard. He tells Max where to find the flour and sugar. He doesn't weigh anything – just chucks the four ingredients into a glass bowl, stirs.

They got up 20 minutes ago – Max was already awake when Adam placed a hand on his shoulder, kissed him on the lips. Then – the excruciating response: Max's eyes flaring wide open; his mumbled, 'Rather not,' as he shrank away from him like plastic thrown into fire.

They eat as soon as the pancakes are wrestled off the pan, taking turns pouring syrup, spooning sugar, rolling them up into tubes, biting.

Afterwards, in the living room, they drink coffee. Adam stares out at the glinting office blocks; between them are slivers of silver sea, and the harbour's cranes.

'Sorry about earlier,' Max says.

Adam turns, forces a smile. 'No worries.'

'Please forgive me. I just... I'm not ready.'

'Really, it's no biggie.' Adam considers telling him he's not really ready either; he considers telling him about Raees. He decides against it: it is easier – less painful – to say nothing. 'What are you getting up to today?'

'Research for my dissertation.' Max stands up. 'I better get going.'

Adam nods. He wants to suggest they hang out a bit more. Or they could meet again later. Even if sex is not going to happen, there is something here, something between them, something he's not ready to let go of.

He unlocks the door, and the security gate which swings open into the corridor. 'Can I get your number?'

Max shakes his head. 'Sorry.'

He grimaces. 'Why not? Have I done something to offend? Would you prefer we never see each other again?'

'You've been nothing but wonderful. I just... My dad will kill me if he knows I wrote the story. I've got to be very careful.'

'What has your number got to do with the story? How would your dad...

I don't get it.'

'I can't tell you. I should never have stayed over. I'm really sorry.'

'What's going on, Max? Why all the cloak-and-dagger *kak*?'

Wincing, Max says, 'My dad's super conservative.'

'Fine, plenty of parents are. But that doesn't explain why you can't give me your number. You're using a pseudonym – how could he possibly find out about the story?'

Max sighs. 'Believe me, there are ways he could. I know I'm sounding paranoid. You just have to trust me on this. I'm really sorry.'

'If you don't want to see me again, then just man up and say so. I'm a big boy; I can take it on the chin. No need to use your fucking father as an excuse.'

Max tightens the grip on his satchel. 'It's not that. It's not that at all. Of course I would try to see you again, if I could.'

Adam shakes his head. 'You're a coward,' he seethes. 'Just tell your dad you're gay; for fuck's sakes, it's 2012!'

'Thanks for the lovely evening,' Max mumbles. 'And the pancakes.'

Adam watches him go down the steps, rueing his outburst, fighting the urge to grab him before he disappears through the gate. Is this it then? He might as well have just been punched in the stomach.

The city is different after the rain: sharper, brighter, cleaner. As Max walks, the details surge out at him – the wrought iron lace of Victorian villas, circular windows on a curvaceous Art Deco block of flats. Two doves coo from a telephone wire. He stops right beneath them, feels the daring wash over him. It isn't wise to turn around, to ascend this hill like he did in the safe dark of last night. It isn't wise – but he is doing it anyway. A breeze broadcasts schoolchildren's cries from an unseen playing field. Otherwise, it is quiet. Back at the gate, he presses the button for flat nine.

'Hello?'

He coughs. 'It's me. Max.'

He's let in. He climbs the stairs, waits for Adam to unlock the security gate.

'Hey.' He's biting his lower lip.

'Hi,' says Adam, arms crossed, refusing to concede a smile.

As soon as Adam has closed the door behind him, Max springs on to him. He is on autopilot now, as Adam almost topples, regains balance. They tussle to the bedroom. When they are both naked, he grabs Adam's hands with his own, pushes him down onto the bed. He does not look down. His dick presses against Adam's stomach, scrapes briefly against his erection, the neat bush of hair. He yelps – he's coming. He lets go of Adam's hands, rolls away onto his back.

'Sorry. I'm so sorry.'

He opens his eyes. Adam is on his haunches, watching him, before getting up, disappearing. Max can hear the sound of a tap running. He goes to the doorway of the bathroom, watches Adam scrubbing the cum off his stomach with the wet corner of a towel.

The words won't come; just a brief quivering, and then tears.

'I'm sorry, I'm sorry,' he eventually manages to whisper.

'What's wrong?' Adam says, chucking the towel into a wicker basket. 'What's there to be sorry about?'

He's guided back to the bed. They sit down together.

'You didn't come. I came so soon. I'm so sorry you didn't come.' He lets the words tumble out; are they making any sense?

'Dude, whatever, that doesn't matter.'

Adam pulls the duvet over him but he continues to shiver. Why did he come back?

'Can I make you some rooibos?'

'Yes, please.'

Adam gets dressed and leaves him. Max is relieved to be on his own. He puts his clothes on. He should not have come back. Why did he come back?

Adam returns with two mugs.

'Thanks so much,' he says, taking the tea.

The bed wheezes as Adam sits down.

'Are you sure you don't want to tell me what the hell is going on?'

Max is gripping the mug with both his hands.

'I can't. It's complicated. I really can't.'

After Max has departed, Adam calls Zandile.

'It's so fucking weird.'

'It's not weird, Adam. It's simple. He's closeted and paranoid.'

'But his phone. Why does he think his dad would know if we texted? That shit is *kak*-weird. And then he was crying straight after he came. He was a wreck. I wish I knew what was going on.'

'He's probably just overwhelmed. Maybe you were his first. Remember your first time? You called me up afterwards, crying, to ask if you could catch

HIV from a hand job!'

'There's something more going on here, I'm convinced. You should've seen him squirm when I asked him last night what inspired his story. I don't think his dad's a businessman. He must be, like, a politician or something. A government or security services type. Someone who could easily find out what he's up to.'

'Maybe, Miss Marple. Maybe. You're jumping to conclusions, though. I bet he's just fearing the worst and being completely paranoid. But – it doesn't matter. He doesn't want to talk. Get over it.'

'I'm tempted to tell him he has to tell us why he's being so darn secretive or we won't publish the story.'

'God, Adam! Don't be so petty. You've never made a stipulation like that for any of our other contributors.'

'But none of the others were James Bond wannabes! Don't we have a right to know why he's being like this? If his caution is any measure, we could be at risk by publishing his work.'

'Now you're the one being paranoid. Come on. Obvs Max is just *poes*-scared his bigoted daddy is going to find out he's a *moffie*. It's not because the story's controversial. In any case – so what if "The President" ruffles a few feathers... isn't that kind of the point?'

Max can't tell anyone, not even the person he wants to tell the most and maybe that – and not what happened those weeks ago – is the worst. He can feel it inside him: tamped and unarticulated for so long, it's growing and morphing without a confession to capture and contain it.

As he approaches the train station, all he can do is walk, and try to breathe, try to be like the cloud unfurling in front of Table Mountain now, steadily blanketing the blue sandstone massif.

Earlier, when Adam was letting him out, he asked if he was sure they couldn't see each other again. Max told him it was better if they didn't. Adam just nodded, sighed like he knew remonstrating would be futile. It feels aeons ago now: the hug – more like a clench – goodbye, the steps to the street. Outside, on the pavement, he had paused for a second, looked up at Adam's flat, but there was no sign of him; he had retreated inside, out of his life. He forced himself to start walking again. It was for the best.

At home, Max pulls his cellphone out of the bedside drawer where he left it yesterday before heading into town. He switches it on. There are two voicemails.

His dad's bark: 'Where are you, Max? I've been trying to get through to you. I want you to come to dinner. Saturday evening. I shall send a car around just before seven.'

He contemplates lying – phoning his dad, telling him he's sick. But his dad will want to know what's wrong with him. And he will only have postponed – not indefinitely deferred – their next meeting. He might as well get it out of the way.

Then, the next recording – 'Max, it's Suraya. I'm worried about you – I haven't been able to get through. Are you OK? Call me when you get this.'

To spare himself being quizzed, he texts her: I'm totally fine. Sorry, mislaid my phone. Coffee tomorrow?

Max has told his dad he'll find his own way to dinner. He goes to Newlands Forest first. Sometimes – often – he goes there with Suraya. But it's unlikely she will want to go when it's storming, and, anyway, he needs to be alone. He sees just one other person – a runner in Day-Glo flashing past him. The families – their zig-zagging dogs and waddling toddlers and snoozing infants – are sensibly at home.

The rain is soft, whispering through the pines, dripping onto his raincoat as he trudges the gravel track. He reaches a clearing, his favourite resting place. It is too wet to sit down on the bench. The city is hidden – there is just deepening grey cloud below him; only the faint whine of a motorbike edging the forest betrays its presence. He wants to carry on walking, up, deeper into the mountain, following the gravel as it shrinks to a narrow strip, curling around contours. Yes, he could go on, groping in the dark until he loses himself, until he slips and falls. But he doesn't. It is nearly seven.

Dinner starts as it always does in winter – with whisky in front of the fire. But this time Max has one too (he normally insists on water). It is Laphroaig: the dirty medicine, like blood and cough mixture, slips between glinting of ice cubes, sears his throat as he swallows faster than he should. His father criticises his hair – he does not like dreads, even pencil-thin ones neatly tamed into a bun like his are. Max is told he is looking too thin, too tired. He is asked how university is going – is he attending all his seminars, handing things in on time?

At least this time he's spared the speech about what a shame he's not studying economics or computer science or something – unlike English literature – his father deems actually useful.

Max stares at the fire, mourns the emptiness of his glass, lets the bass voice thunder unimpeded – like he's tolerating an ocean's incoming tide. To avoid the risk of censure, he need only offer his dad the occasional grunt, an assent, some sign of receipt; this is a lecture, after all – a transmission rather than an exchange.

At about 7.20pm, the door opens, and Vusi, the butler, comes in with a woman. Her auburn hair is a little wet, her pale cheeks are flushed; she must have hung her coat up in the hallway because she is wearing just a tweed skirt nudging her knees, and a grey silk blouse. She apologises for being late. Max's dad is smiling as he rises slowly from his armchair. He takes her hand in both of his. 'I want you to meet my son, Max.'

She and Max shake hands. 'This is Georgina Phillips,' Max's dad says. 'You two might even have crossed paths before – she's a professor at your university.'

Max nods. 'What field?'

'Gender Studies.'

He nods again, glances from her to his dad, who is still smiling. He is wondering how they met; are they fucking? Vusi is hovering by the door. Max's dad offers Georgina a drink; she asks for a glass of Chardonnay and Vusi disappears with a nod. When he returns with the bottle, Max notices it's from the winery that Adam and Zandile do the branding for.

'Why are you smiling like that?' barks Max's dad.

Max looks at him. He was smiling?

'I'm not sure.'

Georgina turns to Max while his dad is in the bathroom. 'Your father is a wonderful man, Max.'

They must be fucking, he thinks. 'Where did you two meet?'

'We've known each other for sometime, actually. I used to head up the Foundation for Rural Women. We made a few presentations to portfolio committee meetings in Parliament; I met him there.'

He nods. That name... he remembers the headlines, right before the last election, wasn't it? There'd been an uproar about what the Foundation was spending its Norwegian grant money on – food parcels distributed at ruling party rallies. The Official Opposition (and some of the spunkier newspaper columnists) had labelled it shameless vote-buying.

'And you're in academia now?'

Georgina nods. 'The foundation closed. Foreign funding dried up. But also,

I think I'm more suited to the university context. My NGO work was very special, but I'm more about policy *development* than implementation, really.'

'I hear you. One can only endure so much of getting one's hands dirty at the grassroots,' he says, staring intently at her manicured nails. 'It's no wonder you retreated up the ivory tower.'

'Well,' she says, blushing, not sure whether Max is mocking her or not.

No one else arrives. Max sits opposite Georgina at the table; his dad sits at its head. Georgina asks him what his dissertation on.

Woolf, he tells her.

'Did you know she was a frightful racist?'

'I'm sure, in the 1920s, your ancestors were too.'

'So why English lit? Did you ever think of studying isiZulu?'

'It's never crossed my mind. For starters, I can barely speak a word of it.'

Georgina almost drops her fork. 'What do you mean? Don't you talk Zulu with your father? I'm sure you two are only speaking English for my benefit.'

He shakes his head. He could explain to her – they've never spoken it to each other; there was never enough time spent together for him to learn it. But he won't bother.

His dad, still chewing, is signalling to Vusi for more Cabernet Sauvignon.

After the malva pudding and Ultra-Mel, Max's dad and Georgina return to the sitting room; Max walks down the passage to the toilet. He stops before he reaches it. The door to his old bedroom (the one he would use during holidays when he was in high school) is open. He leans against the doorway. An outside light shimmers through the big sash window, spilling over chunks of the bed like milk. The shelf is empty of his books; he removed all of them when he first began university. Nothing of his remains, not even a forgotten soft toy – it's like he's never lived here.

When he returns from pissing, he notices Georgina has discarded her stiletto heels; her slim legs are folded elegantly beneath herself on the couch. She is laughing; she turns away when she sees him, her face flushing like a schoolgirl caught bunking.

Yes, yes: they are definitely fucking.

His father looks up, squinting at Max through the swirling cigar's smoke.

'Brandy?' asks his dad.

'No thanks. I'm off,' he announces to them both. 'Thanks for dinner.'

Outside, dying leaves scent the cold night air. Max breathes in until his lungs are bursting, then exhales like it's the first time he's exhaled all evening.

Jaco has opened the sachet; the brownish crystals are caught by the car's overhead light. 'Just dab it round your gums,' he tells Adam, who watches Jaco lick his pinkie and slide it into the plastic. A few granules stick to his finger; he pulls it out, swipes below his lip. Adam copies him. He scrunches up his face – the granules taste sour – and takes a swig from Jaco's water bottle.

There is nothing at first – nothing while they walk from the car to the queue, while they wait, shuffling forward, while they pay and get their wrists stamped. Slow, warm stirrings of something as they climb the stairs, music blooming towards them, and then onto a dance-floor swirling with colour and light. They wind between the bodies. Jaco orders them tequila shots and vodka lemonades.

Adam doesn't want either – he wants a beer – but this is Jaco's world and Jaco's night and so he will just follow. Anyway, now there is not so much acquiescence as peace: he'll down those drinks and they'll go and dance, catching waves of sound, riding the flow of beats through their bodies, the past and future wordlessly melting away (for the time being at least).

Jaco introduces him to Bradley, an older guy, probably 40, sexy – gymmed body in a white V-neck. He is talking to him but it is too loud. Adam laughs in agreement anyway. Jaco throws an arm round him as they dance. 'Having fun?' he roars and Adam nods emphatically. He follows him towards the balcony. To his right he sees Raees and his heart surges, then falls. Of course it's not! Raees hasn't lived in Cape Town in months and, anyway, wouldn't be seen dead in a gay club.

A joint is passed around outside. Bradley looks at him, hands it over; their fingers touch.

Adam, lying still fully clothed on his bed, stares out the window. It has stopped raining; the city beyond the glass is slickly shimmering. He doesn't know what time it is – his phone's battery is dead. And even if it weren't, it's not like he could call him. Not Raees, certainly not Bradley. Him – Max. Where is he now? Where does he live?

He wishes he could hold him, wants to fall asleep right next to him, only him, if only – yes, if only he were here.

SUNDAY

[6]

Imagine Max could just tell her – if he could just say: Suraya, I met this boy, an editor; he's publishing a story I've written about a gay president; and I really, really like him. But he can't tell her that – it is stupid to even wish he could. It is not that she can't be trusted. But ignorance is just safer, easier – even the most discreet can let secrets slip out.

They are sitting in Starlings' rear garden both wrapped up in scarves and coats, clutching their flat whites with both hands.

She lets go of her cup, squeezes his forearm.

'I'm so glad we're doing this. It feels like we haven't hung out in ages.' Her face grows serious. 'Has everything been OK lately?'

'Yes. Absolutely. Why?'

'I can't quite put my finger on it. You've just seemed a bit preoccupied I suppose. And then I began freaking out when I couldn't reach you on Friday.'

'Oh, yes, I had mislaid my phone. I found it again, though. I'm 100% fine, promise!'

'If there's something wrong, you can tell me, hey? I'm here for you. You can tell me anything, friend.'

Shit. What does she suspect? His heart is beating faster. 'Thanks, hon. I really appreciate that.'

30 Rock is all Max can face tonight, and even that is too abrasive, too silly; he forsakes it after just one episode. He wonders where Adam is, what he's doing, who he's with. He wonders how indiscriminately Adam deploys that grin – that sleepy, sloppy, grin with a head tilted to one side, eyes closed when they weren't gazing at you gently, intently, patiently. How many boys (or boys *and* girls) beelined to his Tamboerskloof flat; how many others were similarly, stupidly beguiled?

Well past midnight, Adam still hasn't fallen asleep and feels no closer to do-ing so. He yanks down his boxers. He is only slightly hard, but the squeezing changes that. There is purpose – he will fall asleep after this; but there is something else: anger, and –

He is thinking about Max, about being inside him. Yes, he'll show the bastard. He thrusts into him from behind, ignores the wincing, fuck it's tight, as tight as he wants it to be. And then he is not thinking about Max. It is Raees – they are in the drunken dark, their first time, and he is throbbing, sinking, falling into him. There are no words, no explanation, just sensation, just wondrous connection, just them.

But – it is just a flash, a synapse, a brutal, brief imagining. All that is long gone. Long fucking gone. And so he doesn't continue. He lets go of his dick, climbs out of bed, washes his hands in the cold bathroom light. He clutches the soap and squeezes so that the bar bends, almost breaks, slipping out of his hands.

He cannot stop himself: on his laptop he logs onto Facebook. He unfriended Raees ages ago, but his profile is open anyway. And there they are – the wedding pictures. Raees's new wife looks pretty and young and maybe a little bit scared. Behind them, a crown of skyscrapers and cranes – Dubai. Family joyously crowds into every picture. He slams shut the computer and goes back to bed.

MONDAY

[7]

Nothing has prepared Max for this – no rules, no handbook to guide him, no mentor to consult. And so he tries to think carefully, weighing up approaches, testing them (hypothetically that is) for risks, downsides, unintended consequences. Thinking, thinking, thinking – to the point where his brain fizzes and sputters and freezes – exhausted.

There was no way of getting hold of Connie that didn't involve phone or internet – concealing their catch-up was impossible. Trying to hide it would backfire; the furtiveness would be suspicious. And so he doesn't bother to.

They meet during Connie's lunch-break. As he approaches the restaurant on St George's Mall, he spots her outside, thumbing her phone while she waits for him. He stops next to a lamppost. His Converse sneakers don't need tying but he crouches down and redoes the laces anyway; it allows him to breathe for a moment, to practice a wide, sunny smile. Right, now he is in character: her former boss's son; the kid who loves reading as much as she did. Of course he can act the part easily, but he's afraid of her seeing the fear he's not able to entirely mask, the way his gaze perpetually, compulsively darts around for signs of surveillance.

The Knife is sharp, Max will give him that. 6.03pm, as he's leaving the bookshop, his shift done, and it's there: a black Mercedes in the loading bay right outside. He starts to walk past it, pretending he doesn't know it's waiting for him. Hooting. He turns. Yes, the limo is hooting now, and its hazards have begun to flash.

He sighs. Wouldn't it have been nice if he'd gotten it wrong, if his paranoia had just been that, if this limo and its impetuous blaring were for someone else? But it is not for someone else, and he knows that. He fights the urge to turn again, to run; but he knows he can't outrun this, he needs to accept whatever is coming next. He walks up to the driver's door; the window is down; a man in a black suit and tie is at the wheel.

'Get in the back.'

Max opens the door. There are no other passengers, and he finds some solace in this.

'Where are we going?' he manages to ask.

The driver does not answer. He switches off the hazards, flicks on the right indicator and nudges into the stream of cars. Max, closing his eyes, exhales.

Max enters through the Mount Nelson's revolving door. He slows down, stops. There is no use in rushing. He sees a huddle of guests checking in at the wood-panelled front desk, walks into the chandelier-studded lounge where guests are still taking afternoon tea. He shakes his head. Was this deliberate? Did The Knife choose for them to meet here, at this very hotel, on purpose?

His hands ball into fists. He unclenches them. He will not think about that night; he will not let it throw him. He walks into the Planet Bar. Max's gaze drifts from the rows of glittering bottles to a wingback armchair. He sees The Knife's head first – its shaven gleam. After the initial flicker – of what, fear? – he's OK. Somehow he'll get through it. Somehow he'll be fine.

The Knife smiles smoothly, squeezes his hand in greeting. He does not offer him drink – instead tells him to sit down next to him before taking a slurp of his own.

'How have you been, boy?' His tone is, as usual, soft and avuncular.

Max mumbled something – he can't recall now what.

'You don't watch porn anymore, I've noticed.'

The Knife's eyes are twinkling. 'Not once on Grindr, either.'

Max shrugs.

'In fact you've been squeaky clean lately, Max. It's almost a little worrying.'

The Knife leans forward and pats him – twice, slowly. 'What are you up to, young man?' The tone hasn't changed – but there was something concealed by it now, a menace. Max's knee is tremoring, burning, even though The Knife is no longer anywhere near it – his palms are steepled together now.

He swallows. 'I'm just getting on with my life. Or trying to. I can't deny it isn't always on my mind, that you're there, that you're watching.'

'Indeed. Like God.'

Max wishes he was brave enough to roll his eyes.

'You met Connie Msimang this afternoon.'

Max inhales. The burn in his knee has jumped up to his face. Is it obvious? Please, God, may it not be.

'I did, yes. She used to be my dad's press officer.'

'So? She hasn't been employed by him for almost two years; most of the time since then she's been an editor at *Sunday Press*. Why did you meet with her?'

'Who used to pick me up at half-term – do you think it was my father?' he snaps. 'Connie and I go back a long way. She was like a big sister to me when I was in boarding school. My only regret is that I haven't made more of an effort to keep in touch. I'm trying to change that. Ever since I started varsity I've been too much inside my head. I'm trying to get better at....'

'I see,' The Knife cut in. 'Well, I hope for your sakes it was purely a social engagement. Because don't think you can run to the press and get away with it.'

Max sighs. 'You know, as well as I do, that Connie doesn't cover news, salacious or otherwise. She edits the culture pages. She wouldn't know what to do with a scoop.'

Smiling, The Knife's palm pressed against Max's knee once more.

'How is Suraya? And her family? You're very fond of her.'

'She's fine.'

'I'm sure you'd like her to stay that way.'

'What do you mean?'

'You know exactly what I mean.' He removes his hand. 'It would be a shame if her father were to find out about the white boy she's fucking, or the abortion she had last year, wouldn't it? An upstanding imam like that would never live it down, would he? Still, I suppose that pales in comparison to the brakes of her car *tragically* failing when she's zooming around Hospital Bend.'

He feels sick. He wishes he had a whisky. They're in a hotel bar – why couldn't The Knife have ordered him a damn whisky?

'I suggest you don't chat to Ms Msimang again. Or anyone else in the media, for that matter. I don't care what their beat is – they could be the paper's crossword puzzle designer or the editor's dog walker for all I care.'

Max stared at The Knife. The seconds slowed. 'First you threatened to tell my dad I'm gay. Now you're threatening to make life difficult – or worse! – for Suraya.' What's next? The question, unvoiced, hangs between them.

Max stands; it shocks him, the daring of just walking away. He doesn't look back. He finds the bathroom, splashes his face with cold water. Adam. He'll go visit Adam! Sense has abandoned him, perhaps – but there is something imperative, essential about going to him, even if he can't articulate why. He wants to be with someone (and it obviously can't be Suraya) – he can't bear to face the horror of The Knife's remarks alone.

Adam dismounts his bike, rummages in his satchel for his keys.

'Adam.'

He almost yelps. Leaning against the tree, mostly in shadow, is Max.

'Fucking hell, you gave me a fright.'

Max steps forward.

Adam squints at him. He wonders if Max has been crying; there is something washed out, harried about his face.

'Are you OK?'

Max's bites his lower lip to stop it from quivering. 'Not really. Do you mind if I come in?'

'I had a horrible encounter this evening. Someone who works with my dad. He was a bit threatening. It shook me up a little.'

'And so you came here.' An observation – not a question.

'Yes.'

'Don't you have friends? People you actually know? People you trust?'

'I knew that if I came here – '

'I'd be stupid enough to let you in?' Adam sighs. 'You're right. I'm a sucker.'

'I didn't mean that. I can't explain it; I know we barely know each other. But I trust you.'

'Bullshit,' says Adam, crossing his arms. 'If you really trusted me, you'd tell me what the hell is going on.'

'It's messy. It's safer for me – and for you – if you don't get involved.'

'If you don't want me involved then why the hell were you waiting for me on my doorstep?'

Max is getting up from the chair. For a moment Adam thinks he's going to leave, but he doesn't, he takes the mug from out of his hands and puts it down on the coffee table.

'Get up.'

Adam stands. He lets Max's hands slide down his arms, lets Max's mouth come close, lets himself be kissed. Max leads him to the bedroom, switches on the lamp like it's his own. Adam kicks off his shoes. He tries not to think, not to hope; the shadows of last time linger, they could swamp them, they probably will.

They are both just in their underwear, shivering.

When they are under the duvet, Max kisses him on the lips, on the soft hair above his sternum; he bites his nipples gently, before beginning a steady descent.

Afterwards, they bath. Adam sits behind Max, swiping a soap bar in semi-circles on his back. They take turns swigging from a whisky bottle.

'You OK?'

Max nods, turns to kiss him.

'I didn't expect this.'

'This what?'

'Us. When I came to make sure you'd got the story. I didn't expect we'd....' He doesn't complete the sentence; and Adam doesn't try to do so for him. Instead, Adam touches a circle of what looks like freshly healed skin on Max's shoulder.

'What happened here?'

Max tries to look over his shoulder, then turns back to face the taps.

'It's nothing.'

He can see Max has tensed up and so he drops it. When they've climbed out, he finds Max a towel, the fluffiest one in the cupboard, and fetches him a pair of boxers and an old T-shirt.

Back in bed, they listen to the rain. There are unformed questions circling Adam's throat, but he ignores these; instead he nuzzles the soapy sweetness of Max's neck. He marvels at the change – there is no stiffening, no tension, but rather a fluidity in the way Max melts back into him.

Adam feels himself hardening again, wonders if Max has noticed. He lets a hand slide under Max's T-shirt, sweeping slowly across his stomach. Max shivers when it reaches his chest, turns onto his back, folding his arms behind him.

Adam brings his hand down, it brushes Max's swelling dick through the cotton, squeezes it. He pulls down the boxers, hears gasping as he takes Max into his mouth.

In the dream, Max is in the Mount Nelson's foyer for the first time, staring at the zebra-striped floor, waiting. A uniformed man doffs his pith helmet and asks him why he's here. Dazedly, he tells him who he's looking for.

The guard smiles, perhaps knowingly, perhaps not; his arm juts out towards the Planet Bar. They are waiting for him under a mobile of twirling, glossy planets – how fitting for two masters of the universe, Max thinks. The Knife grips his hand tightly, shakes it, and then turns to the other man, short and fat and balding. A waiter comes up, takes drinks orders; Max requests the same as The Knife and his Canadian friend: a double Johnny Walker Blue on ice. The conversation is polite and inconsequential, barely heard above the beating of his heart. He watches the man opposite, observes the discreet blue tie, the shinier-than-coal shoes, the glinting wedding band and Rolex, the hands fluttering like fleshy moths.

Max wants to scream, to run. He drains his whisky, puts the tumbler down, motions for another. Too soon, The Knife is standing up and smiling and saying goodbye to them both. Now Max is alone with the salivating, triumphant Canadian. He invites Max to accompany him. They silently stand together, close but not touching. The doors open. Max follows the man's shuffle down the empty corridor. A key card is tapped; the door to the suite opens; Max is ushered inside. The light in the anteroom is soft; it is brighter in the bedroom where a dazzling white bath towel has been spread out on the king bed. Thick curtains keep the world at bay, the hotel's famous gardens hidden. He smells the whisky-breath, cologne – the same fragrance his father loves to wear.

'Call me "daddy",' drawls the Canadian. The mustache hovering against Max's ear is making him squirm. A hand snakes down to to his arse, squeezing it so hard he yelps. He falls silent again. No point in abusing his vocal chords – the soundproofing here is most likely five-star.

Adam holds Max tightly, silently, letting him weep.

'It's OK,' he says. 'You're safe.'

He put the light on earlier, when he was woken by Max's whimpering. He shook him when he yelled – something unintelligible, not words, just feelings. Then Max's eyes shot open; his mouth clamped shut.

Adam loosens his hands. 'Why don't I make us some rooibos?'

Max sniffs. 'Thank you,' he croaks. He's sitting cross-legged, tears wiped away, when Adam returns with mugs.

'What were you dreaming about?'

'It wasn't very pleasant.'

'Oh, so this is just one of those things we're just not going to discuss.'

Max takes a sip from his mug. 'Thanks for the tea.'

Adam shakes his head, almost laughs. 'You're welcome, Max. You're bloody welcome.'

When they climb back into bed, Adam doesn't try to cuddle him; he lies on his side, facing the window. The warmth of the rooibos has woken him; he feels too alert, worries that he won't be able to get back to sleep. He needs to be fresh tomorrow – he has to revise a winery press release; the brand manager wants the new version by noon. He sighs. He feels the mattress shifting, feels Max twisting, and then suddenly his chest against his back. Max's fingers stroke his forearm, then drop down.

'Adam.'

Max bites his lip. He's so close to telling, he dearly wants to – but the risk that Adam lets something slip is just too great. The Knife can't know the story is his.

Adam, glaring into the dark, issues, finally, a terse 'Yes? What?'

Nothing. And then: 'Thank you.'

Adam finds Max's hand, lets his fingers trace patterns on it. 'Not at all,' he yawns.

Adam's eyes flash open. He is on his back. He rolls towards the bed's empty centre. Where the fuck is Max? A panicked fumble with the light switch. Blinking, he climbs out of bed. The living room is empty, so he checks the kitchen. Ah! Max is standing in front of the sink, completely still.

'Sorry – thirsty.' Max fills a glass with water, walks up to Adam. A kiss on the shoulder. Adam grins.

'Come, it's cold,' says Max. 'Let's snuggle.'

TUESDAY

[8]

Adam smiles as he sits down in front of his computer at the office. He doesn't begin work on the press release immediately. Instead he thinks about this morning, about how they woke together, how they showered together, how they stood in the hallway when he was about to go. Max tilted his head, kissed him. They held each other for at least a minute.

Spicy. Fruit-driven. Complex layers of smoky oak surrendering – no, not surrendering – yielding to…

The cursor flashes. He checks his watch. 7.06pm. He needs to get this finished before he goes home. His phone is ringing.

'Did you see my email?'

'Hello, Lindiwe.'

'Did you watch it?'

'Watch what?'

Zandile's mother sighs. 'I emailed you a YouTube clip.'

'I've been working on some deadlines this afternoon. What is it?'

'Just watch it.'

She's put down the phone. Adam opens up his emails, finds hers (it's in his Junk Mail folder), clicks on the link.

The heading below the video player says: Gays to be banned?. The image, slightly grainy, is of a man in a suit standing at a podium. Adam clicks play. He recognises the man; he's seen him in the papers before – it's Richard Lindela, the Minister of Traditional Affairs. He is praising the constitution – 'a framework for our liberation, a map of freedom guiding our course'. And then he declares that it has been 'abused by certain people – a decadent minority with un-African values who seek to corrupt our communities with their unnatural tendencies'.

'That is where the constitution has failed. By indulging a minority, it has trampled on the respect of the majority. Their behaviour is an affront to the dignity of our noble communities. It is dangerous.'

'Unacceptable!' he thunders. 'It is unacceptable for our culture to be disrespected and abused. The constitution must be modified. It is a wonderful document. But we cannot let the people be disrespected by its tolerance for those who are intolerant of our precious values.'

The minister clears his throat, lets his fingers briefly cup his grey goatee. Then he stares ahead – as if he is staring at Adam. He is proposing a way forward. Practical steps to lead to the establishment of a commission that will determine a way of containing this problem so that the dignity and values of the nation can be protected and upheld.

'If this means that certain deviant practices are made illegal, then we must accept this,' he says.

The minister returns to his seat. His compatriots in the ruling party benches are clapping wildly. On the other side of the National Assembly, the Opposition's members are yelling and booing, like supporters of a losing team at a rugby derby. The clip fades.

For a few seconds Adam just stares at the screen. He grabs his phone, dials Zandile.

'What's up? Can we chat later? I'm just about to put dinner in the oven.'

'Have you seen what this minister said this afternoon in Parliament?'

'What?'

'Richard Lindela. He wants to ban homosexuality. I mean he hasn't said so explicitly. But that's basically what he's threatening.'

There's scraping – perhaps she's putting a pot down on a rack.

'Ad, are you sure?'

'Watch the clip. Your mom emailed it to both of us. It's fucking crazy. I think we should run –' He catches himself. He had almost said 'Max's story'. 'I think we should run the Gabriel Roberts story instead of "The Stolen Empire" on Friday.'

'Your boyfriend's going to have to wait,' she smirks. 'I haven't started on the illustration for "The President" yet.'

'Come on!'

There's a pause. 'You're right. You're absolutely right. I'll come in early tomorrow and get it done then. I was going to keep the design quite simple anyway.'

When they've finished, he watches the clip again. He calls Lindiwe.

She answers after the second ring.

'I watched it.'

'You need to run that story,' she says. 'That story Zandile told me about, the one about the gay president.'

'I know. I've just been telling Zandile that.'

'It's disgusting.' Her voice is hoarse. 'We need to fight this.'

Adam Googles: richard lindela gay rights speech. A wire agency's article is up on a few news websites. Minister calls for gay rights rethink is the one headline used; for the same article, Gay ban mooted is another. It is a short piece – only quoting from the minister's speech. No effort has been made to procure comment from other sources: there is no spluttering LGBT activist or gloating tribal chief.

On the presidency's website there's a press statement headed Approach to rights remains unchanged. The statement says the president 'takes note' of the comments made in the National Assembly by the Right Honourable Minister Richard Lindela. In 'a vibrant democracy and a vibrant party, alternative views and dialogue is encouraged' it says. The president 'still believes that the constitutional safeguards provided to the LGBT community should be protected. However, the president commends our comrade's willingness to open a discussion on the relevance of these rights and their impact on societal values and looks forward to observing the deliberations around this.'

Adam checks Twitter. @aardwolf73, a gay blogger with about 2,300 followers, has shared the link to one of the syndicated news articles. WTF! We going to ban gays now?! and then, two minutes later: Wake up, people! The ruling party wants to ban gays.

There are a few replies to him. Stop being so dramatic. Typical gay ;-) this is just a dialogue.

@aardwolf73 replies: I've been told I'm a deviant and don't belong in this country. #hardlydramatic

Adam goes onto the Official Opposition party's website. Today's only new media release is a statement bemoaning the increased unemployment rate. He checks its leader's Twitter feed. Meeting with Berlin mayor went well is her most recent tweet, posted a few hours ago. There is a picture of her chewing on a bratwurst next to a beaming, grey-haired man.

He wonders if Max knows about what happened in Parliament this morning. He wishes he could speak to him now.

Adam is staring at the red traffic light, waiting with one foot on the road, the other on his bicycle's pedal, when it first occurs to him. *Max.* What if Max knew that the minister was going to make this speech? Maybe he knew Minister Lindela; maybe they were related; maybe he knew this was going to happen. He wants to pull his bike onto the pavement, next to the Chinese takeaway, and call Zandile. But it is green now, and he can't tell Zandile on the phone, can he – not if he wants to talk about Max.

His mouth is dry. His heart is beating fast. It is not just from the pedalling. He wishes he could find Max now, wishes he could ask him. When another set of lights change to red, he brakes, climbs the kerb. He calls Lindiwe. She's at home.

'To what do I owe the honour,' grins Lindiwe after they've they both sat down in her living room.

'It's this story. "The President".'

'Wait, you haven't published it yet? Better strike while the iron's hot, Adam. This country needs this kind of provocative art – now more than ever.'

'Did Zandile tell you about the guy who wrote it?'

She shakes her head.

'He's absolutely terrified he'll be found out by his dad. We don't communicate on telephone or email – he's that paranoid.'

'Clearly in Narnia still, shame.'

'I've been thinking – well, I've thought it all along: unless you're a complete nutcase, you can only be scared of your dad finding out through phone and email, surely, if he's somehow related to government or the security services.'

She nods. 'I suppose that's fair. But it isn't necessarily the case. Being in the closet can easily warp your sense of reality – didn't you find that?'

Adam looks at her. Before he came out to his parents in his first year of college he'd been a little secretive and ashamed, sure, but he certainly hadn't suspected they were bugging his phone, or hacking into his email.

'What if the writer isn't any old run-of-the-mill closet case? What if he's, I don't know, like the minister's son? He probably knew this was going to happen. That's why he wrote it, and sent it to us. As a form of protest. He wrote "The President" because he's angry about what they're doing. But he doesn't want them – or us – to know it was him.'

'And...?'

He hesitates. She doesn't seem at all fazed by this possibility.

'I'm not sure if Richard Lindela has any offspring though given the close attention he would pay those poor typists in the Congress's Lusaka office; it's not impossible, I suppose.' Her eyeballs drift upwards as she scans her memories. 'But it honestly doesn't matter, Adam. It doesn't matter whether the author is a minister's son, whether he's even the president's son for God's sake. His story stands on its own.'

'But – and this is what I wanted to ask you about – if he's so scared... are we, as publisher, in danger?'

'Of course not. It's just a short story, Adam. Even if they did find out that it was one of their own – what would they do? It's a free country. Trust me, I know these people. The boy is just worried about his daddy turfing him out of the house.'

WEDNESDAY

[9]

Adam can't sleep and so, just after six, he climbs out of bed and gets dressed. At some point in the night the reassurance he'd felt from talking to Lindiwe – a calm, measured certainty – had all but vanished. Lindiwe is wise, principled, smart; if she thinks they should publish Max's story – and that doing so wouldn't be dangerous – then that's exactly what they must do. This doubt – this is nerves, he tells himself. He needs to run them away.

He does not head onto the mountain's jagged darkness; he lets the wind tug him down the hill, lets the streetlights guide him into the city's centre.

On Adderley Street, the flower sellers have already started arranging their arums and proteas. A hawker pushes a curio-stuffed cart past them; it teeters as it overcomes the kerb, so Adam helps to steady it before continuing. He can smell croissants as he passes a bakery; inside there are only two patrons, both nursing coffees. He wishes he had drunk one before he setting off.

He looks up at the buildings. Some floors are seamed with light, others are blank as pages. Branches flicker out over him. Cars occasionally surge past. Finally, he notices the lampposts. *Daily Sun*, the country's biggest tabloid, has posters up advertising stories from today's edition.

The first he passes declares:

MY DINNER WITH A TOKOLOSHE

The next:

DAD 'RAPES' INFANT TWICE

And then the third poster:

'BAN THE HOMOS' URGES MINISTER

It is made real then – to see it in ink, the screaming sans serif capitals. What happened to this beloved country, the supposedly New South Africa, Tutu's 'rainbow nation'? Where are they living now?

Adam takes comfort in these things: the triumph of the office's lamps over the windows' darkness; Zandile in front of her computer; Miriam Makeba exhorting them, through the Bluetooth speakers, to 'meet me at the river'.

Another online search yields little. On *Business Day*'s website, he finds a short report by the paper's parliamentary correspondent quoting the President's statement and a constitutional law expert who warns that, although it would be unlikely for the constitution to change, the comments made by Richard Lindela could have serious implications – particularly in hardening attitudes towards sexual minorities.

There is nothing on *RainbowCentral*, the gay news site – the most recent news story is Why Miley is the Ultimate Fag Hag. WTF!

'Check out *New Era*,' says Zandile, pointing at her screen. 'They've just run an opinion piece about it. You know who owns it, right?'

'I might not have your illustrious Struggle pedigree, but I'm not a total ignoramus about who's running the country. *New Era* is owned by that billionaire businessman who the president's very pally with.'

'Indeed! Look at you, being all informed,' she chuckles. 'So, it won't then surprise you to hear the screed they've published.' She starts reading from the op-ed: 'Finally, common sense is emerging on the matter of the gays. It has been for far too long that the rights of the majority have been ignored to serve the interests of corrupt, white depravity which has no place in our current dispensation of freedom.'

'Jeez. Who wrote that shit?'

'The chair of the Congress Youth League. Listen to this. 'We will mobilise our structures to endorse Comrade Lindela's ambitions to create dialogue around this, and his bid to implement a commission that can come to a satisfactory resolution to ensure freedom for all and a protection of our values.'

'Doesn't 'mobilising structures' typically mean pelting rocks at people?'

'I doubt it's going to come to all that,' says Zandile. 'It's just hot air. Previous youth leaders have demanded 'One settler, one bullet'; others said they would kill for the president. But in the end, pretty much all of it fades into nothing. They're all fart, no poo.'

She shows him the illustration she's been working on to accompany the story. It is a pattern – almost herringbone – in yellow, green and black: the colours of the ruling party. 'What do you think? We need something quite simple and abstract to accompany the piece – no dicks, nothing on the nose.'

'I like it.' Adam returns to his desk. Max's story has already been saved in the back end of *Vula* website. He will read it again now, checking for any spelling or grammar mistakes. They will publish it tomorrow, Thursday – the day they always publish a story.

He shivers. Of course he can't be cold; there's a heater below his desk blasting hot air at his knees. What is it – this on-the-edge-of-an-icy-pool feeling? Is it because of Max – his furtiveness, his fear? Is it the newspaper posters he saw this morning? He wishes it could just happen, that the story can be published and forgotten about, that life can carry on.

He views the Opposition's website again. No media statements have been published since he checked earlier. Idiots! He pulls out his phone – Thabiso's number is still there, undeleted. Gritting his teeth, he begins to dial.

*

Suraya taps Max's arm as they leave the seminar room, but waits for the crowds of students in the corridor to thin before she says, 'I heard on the news, they want to ban homosexual acts. A minister, somebody Richards, is suggesting it?'

Max looks at her as blankly as he can. 'Lindela. Richard Lindela. Wants to set up a commission to advise on whether gay rights should be repealed. I heard that too.'

She grabs his arm. 'Don't you think it's beastly?'

He allows himself to nod. He looks at his Swatch. He wants to smile because he remembers – Adam has the same model, a grey version of the blue one he has.

'Are you going to fight this?' she asks eventually.

'What?' he replies, playing dumb.

'This gay ban thing.'

He looks at her, and then the wave comes; he is not expecting it as it drenches him, as it tugs at him and he crumples.

'I've got to go,' he mumbles. As he strides away, he lets himself cry, lets the campus become blurry, the other students just blobs swimming past. His phone is ringing. It's Suraya. He does not answer her call.

Adam is standing outside Parliament at a secondary gate, not the big main one. There are no limos, no flashing lights here. The solitary policeman on duty glares at him as he waits. Researchers trickle out for lunch. The portly agriculture minister – the only cabinet member known for refusing the protection of a bodyguard – walks past, head down, reading his phone.

'Hey.'

Adam turns around; Thabiso has grabbed his upper arm. He looks different: the dreads and wispy beard have gone; his hair is short; he's wearing tapered chinos, a jacket, a dark tie. But the smile is the same – that cheeky, knowing, once-irresistible smile. He feels a tug. Why did they stop talking again? Their hands reach forward as they both try to figure out whether they should hug. They end up shaking hands.

'Hi.'

Adam smiles. 'How's it going?'

'Surprised, to be honest. Last time I saw you, you told me I should rot in hell. That you never wanted to see me again. Remember?'

Adam shudders, reddening. 'I was a tad precocious back then, wasn't I?

Can you even remember what we were fighting about?'

'Nope. But I probably wanted to stay out late and you wanted to go home. You always peaked early.'

Adam laughs. 'Except when we were fucking. I seem to recall it was more the other way round then.'

'*Eina*. Have you had lunch?'

Adam nods.

'Well, I haven't. I'm going to faint if I don't deep throat a panini in the next three minutes. Walk with me. What's up? I assume you didn't reach out just so you could insult me in person.'

'I wanted to ask you about the anti-gay speech in Parliament yesterday.'

'Not my party, not my problem,' smirks Thabiso. 'Come on. The homophobes – they're on the other side of the aisle. You should be going on a lunch date with Minister Lindela, not me, if you want to complain about that diatribe of his.'

'But you haven't put out a statement reacting to the speech. I've been checking all morning. And – *fokol*. When are you guys releasing something?'

'A decision was made not to.'

'What?'

'Look, it's clear Minister Lindela is just posturing, sucking up to the bigots. And it's not like this is the official Congress position.'

'Even so, though, he carries clout. Why isn't the Alliance for Change condemning it loud and clear?'

'Dude, elections are in less than six months. We're trying our hardest to break new ground with the electorate. And our focus groups show – '

'That standing up for gay rights isn't a vote winner?'

'Pretty much. I mean of course the Official Opposition remains an ardent protector of the rights of all. You and I both know we're super faggot-friendly. Remember my dinner parties... the Alliance is *riddled* with homos. We just don't need to vocalise it at every opportunity. We don't want to be seen as completely out of sync with traditional values.'

Adam shakes his head, his shock burnt up by anger. 'Come on,' he hisses, trying really hard to keep his voice low. 'If you don't speak out against the minister, you're basically agreeing with him. You're condoning his view that homosexuality is some vile deviance, imported by the colonists along with their penal code.'

'You don't get it,' sighs Thabiso. 'Plenty of people are sick of the ruling party; they want an alternative. But they're not going to vote for an alternative that's waving a rainbow flag. It doesn't matter that faggotry is as African as the baobab, that people have been queering it up here since forever. That's historically accurate, sure, but the Opposition is not going to shout that from the rooftops – because too many old school folks have bought into this idea that being gay is some decadent foreign thing.'

'Your party is on a very slippery slope.'

'No, we're not. We're being pragmatic.'

Thabiso's grin has gone. He's not irresistible. He's smug and pompous and verbose, and Adam's sick of him but doesn't walk away from him yet. He doesn't interrupt. Instead, he lets Thabiso's speechifying roll over him. 'We don't want to be stuck as the Opposition forever,' Thabiso is saying. 'The best hope for advancing and protecting constitutionalism will be if the Alliance trounces the Congress and we go into coalition with like-minded partners. But to get enough votes for that – we've got to stop scoring own goals. No more alienating potential voters. We need to be less combative. More conciliatory. And that, sweetpea, means being much more sensitive to this country's social norms.'

THURSDAY

[10]

At the public library, orchestral music (something melancholy and familiar), is playing on the speakers. Max finds a free computer, looks around. There is no one in sight. He sits down, opens the browser, goes to *Vula*'s website.

It is there, on the homepage. "The President". He clicks on the heading. It takes him to the story. He looks down at his left hand, realises he is clenching the chair. He lets go, and starts reading his story as if he has never read it before.

THE
PRESIDENT

By Gabriel Roberts

You are walking along the red corridor. The security guards have frisked you; your small bag has been rammed through an x-ray machine. You have not been told. You do not expect me – I can see this when I take your soft hand and shake it; you don't know how to do it the traditional way, but I forgive you. I go to the drinks cabinet and pour us both whiskies; you are standing, watching me pour the Lagavulin on ice which crackles. I tell you to sit down on the wingback armchair, the only chair.

I go next to the fire, and sit on the springbok skin rug. You finish your drink faster than I do, and I take it and pour another, topping up my own.

You are not stupid, but even you can't imagine what happens next, when I take your emptied glass and pull you up with my one hand. We are standing close. You are looking down now, at my erection. I let go of your hand. I take off my blazer. I tell you to take your hoodie off – and for a moment I am angry: who comes here wearing a hoodie? Not even my grandchildren would dare. But I had asked that you be athletic, and perhaps this is what you were told to wear. I stare at the grey vest, at your protruding, bold biceps. I put my hand on the hardness of your chest for a moment, take it back.

You are still, though your hands are shaking. Your skin is pale; there are tiny lines around the eyes. I would have preferred someone still at school. You're old enough to have a degree at least, but I doubt that you have one – I imagine your life (like mine) didn't allow for this.

I tell you to strip, and you do so silently. First the belt: you tug it, it snares, you tug more forcefully. And then your vest; I gasp a little. There is a trail of hair from sternum to waist, and a furry halo around each brown nipple. And near the belly button, a small dark mole. You pull off your sneakers quickly, socks, too, and then slow down, taking your time with your pants, you fucking tease. When they're around your ankles, you bend down and pull them off inelegantly and stand free, hands finding comfort from your sides. I stare at the little white briefs, and the bulge in their centre, and I wonder, but no, you can't be hard, or are you finally – you know who I am, even a dumb pretty boy like you and maybe that is something.

I ask if you want another drink and pour more whisky, gulping mine as I hand you yours. I sit down in the chair, tell you to join me. You approach slowly from the side, suddenly you're in my lap, wriggling, bum settling on my erection, feet folding over the arm of the chair. The cotton is slightly sweaty. My finger probes the waistband, lets it snap back;

I slide a hand along your smooth back, my fingers mapping the constellation of moles.

We kiss. You taste of whisky and something else, liquorice, maybe, or toothpaste. You tug my lips softly, lick my front teeth. I push you off, pull off the golf shirt from last year's national policy conference, the suit trousers, the shoes and socks.

We are both standing again, close. Your hand touches my belly, traces the blank folds; when it reaches my left nipple I shudder and push your hand away. You frown. I pull your underpants down now and your dick, circumcised, leaps out.

It is only slightly hard, and I hate you for this, I crouch down and angrily suck it, almost bite it, my teeth are touching flesh and you flinch so I lick more gently, I forgive you and taste the cleanness, tongue conversing with the bump of the glans.

Your hands flutter onto my head. Are you mocking the baldness? I do not ask; I just let go, climb upwards dizzily.

My hands sweep down your arms, leave your body, return to your buttocks which I squeeze. These are even paler than the rest of you, incandescent moons in the gloom. I kiss your neck, descend to mark each nob of your spinal column with my lips. I spread open your cheeks, lick the sweatiness tinged slightly with shit, tongue flickering upwards so quickly that you shiver.

I tell you to lie down. Your hand quickly holds your dick: I can see this nearly hidden movement. You turn around and hunch down and then you're on the springbok skin, lolling, balls not quite touching the floor. I squeeze your dick and it resists me proudly.

I let go, walking to the cabinet against the wall where the headband is. Stroke its leopard fur. You watch me, your eyes lidded. You are waiting. I crouch down, place it gently on your head. My warrior, my little warrior. I nearly kiss you on the forehead, but I do not. Instead, I realise I have flipped you over and am lying on you. You breathe stolen breaths, you are almost crumpled as your body interrupts my meeting with the floor. My dick rests in the gap between your buttocks. My warrior. I fall sideways, tell you to get lube which your retrieve from your bag with a hand towel and condoms. I take the little foil squares smiling, watch my hands throw them into the fire. You say nothing. Instead, you pick up your drink, finish the mouthful that remains and return to me.

I lie down, let my legs flop outwards. There is the sound of the bottle cap opening, the slapping of the lube on your dick, and the coolness as you lather it around my arsehole. You push one finger in; the invasion, distantly familiar, shocks me. I relax as another finger joins it. They remove themselves slickly, and after a brief pause, when you stoop to kiss my shoulder blades, it is something else, more emphatic and brutal, that enters me.

Afterwards, after you have left, and I have shat out shit and blood and pain and semen and have clothed myself, and reached the bedroom, after the goodnight to my wife, after my eyes have closed, after sleep bumpily yanks me away from here – after this all there are just dreams and memories and ghosts. They do not let me rest.

You are – where are you? Already gone? Did you know, of course you didn't, you should've known on the march to the helicopter, and when it rose above the kraal, its light bouncing off ancient hills, you should've known as it flew towards the ocean that the guard next to you would be opening the door at 1,000 metres and you would be nudged towards the moon, falling, falling to the black Indian.

That is the way it must be of course. In my dreams I weep for you, for the touch and that second of lips on neck and your hold on my chest. But that is the way it must be.

In my dreams I meet him again, my cousin, and we are in the sugar cane again like the past hasn't happened, and we are wrestling, and falling into the water and he is touching me, the first time, the beginning.

It is always like this, in the rare aftermath: he visits me, oh ghoul, oh spirit, oh demon – he visits me in the fields and he touches my pain, and he plunges, plunges and white splatters against the sharp green leaves as I yell. He disappears, reappearing sliced and crumpled, eyeballs staring up at me, their gaze burning always. Oh that day, when the others knew about him (how did they know?), but they didn't know about me. Oh that day, my friends chasing him. I run with them too. We are younger, faster, we have stones which we throw and they hit him and they fall to the wet, brown earth which reddens as he slows, stops. When he is on the ground, wriggling like a caught fish, when the boys are yelling, when my mouth is yelling too, my heart is exploding with love and hate and fear – that is when he is staring at me. I look at me. In this dream, this always-dream, I turn away, to the clearing where my wives are watching too. They sit, they know, they do not have words or faces, just knowledge – and I hate them. I slash at them, the blood pours like battle, but still they sit and witness. My heart is on fire, unquenchable, raging, hell. And I scream, running forward, running forward, chasing the helicopter that has dispatched you, envying your end.

FRIDAY

[11]

Adam checks the website. Nothing is amiss – and why would it be? He should've known all would be OK. In 24 hours, "The President" has been shared a mere 28 times on Facebook. What's going on, have those fucks changed their algorithm again?

He Googles the president gabriel roberts. His heart sinks: the only relevant search result is RainbowCentral.co.za where a brief post links to the story:

THE 'GAY' PRESIDENT!

Check out this sexy short story by Gabriel Roberts
on Vula imagining if South Africa had a gay president.
A must-read!

'Better than nothing,' he mutters. But a queer news aggregator is hardly the prime time, is it?

'What?' asks Zandile, clicking away at the computer next to him.

'Nothing.'

He searches Twitter next. @aardwolf73 has tweeted, Mzansi's president goes gay. #HAWT with the link. And then later: Big ups to @readVula for publishing "The President" – cheeky short story. Both have been retweeted and favourited a few times.

"The President" has made barely a ripple, in other words.

He swivels to face Zandile. 'You know, that rhino poaching story we published last week made a much bigger splash.' He's not relieved, like he thought he would be. No: he's disappointed. Why is no one reading it, sharing it, arguing over it? Why does no one care?

SATURDAY

[12]

Adam pays for his ticket to Kirstenbosch at its entrance and starts walking quickly. Aside from the clouds huddling against the purple mass of Table Mountain behind him, the sky is clear. Tourists are dotted along the botanical garden's brick pathways, some reading the information boards, others clutching at leaves or branches and inspecting them carefully. A Japanese couple look up at an oak tree, following their guide's pointed arm. An owl stares back at them impassively.

Adam steps through the cycad garden, down into the glen. The trees surge up over him. He gets to Colonel Bird's Bath, a small, circular pool. There is no one there. He sits down on the stone barrier which bars visitors from getting too close. He hears voices – German, possibly – muffled by moss and leaves and the progress of water. They fade away. He wishes he had brought a book to read. He looks at his watch. 12.08pm. It would be impossibly wonderful for Max to appear, for him to actually come here. He remembers the look, the hesitation – or was it just fear? – when he suggested this rendezvous as they were saying goodbye to each other at the flat on Tuesday. The acceptance was cautious, almost begrudging. Why had he suggested Kirstenbosch anyway? Because he is sentimental; because it his favourite place; because he has been coming here since he was a little boy. He brought Raees here, here to this very spot; and maybe that's what he's doing too – reclaiming it for himself, for the future, for a future that maybe, hopefully, could include Max.

He thinks about that day – they just came once here. Raees was preoccupied, biting his fingernails, glancing around constantly. Here, in the shadows by the water, he relaxed a bit until Adam tried to take his hand; he flung it away, stomped off, up into the sunlight.

'Hey.'

Adam looks up. Max is standing in front of him, hands in pockets. They hug, disentangle, smiling at each other. Max clears his throat, mumbles, 'I won't be able to stay for very long, sadly. I can't be certain I wasn't followed.'

Adam stares at him, incredulous, but Max refuses to make eye contact.

'Why bother coming then?'

'To see you. To say goodbye. I'm leaving town for a bit.'

Max turns, steps onto a path tracing the water's gurgling descent from the pool. Adam follows him. The path turns, dips down. They step on raised, dry stones to cross the stream, following the path as it continues up the bank on the other side. Max sees people ahead. Freezes. Adam will never forget that look – the terror. It subsides. Max is forcing himself to continue, he can see that.

'Just stop. Please,' he begs, grabbing Max's sleeve. 'Listen, I wanted to ask – is your surname Lindela? Is that minister – Richard Lindela – your dad?'

Max turns, uses his free hand to shake off Adam's grip.

'I don't know who you're talking about,' mutters Max. He starts walking again; there are steps up towards the lawn, the light. Adam follows him. When they reach the grass, Max says, 'Please, Adam. Wait here a few minutes. Please. *Please* – you have to let me go.'

Max has been walking, hiding, breathing – and now he is at home, blistered and cold, filling a tumbler with whisky he bought en route.

Newlands Forest helped, like it always did. The whirling in his brain slowed as he walked higher, deeper, swallowed up by the shadows, the quiet.

He gulps down a neat mouthful, coughs, almost choking as it incinerates his throat.

He could stand back, on those slopes, could stand back from himself and for a moment watch: mad Max, coiled up in fear, trying to think of everything, all the angles. Enough. He can't think of everything. He knows that, as he takes another, slower, smaller sip. The burn is the same; he can feel it warming him, seeping towards his fingers. Maybe the cab was being followed earlier; maybe it wasn't. There's no use in fretting over it.

Poor Adam. He can still feel the anger – it had radiated from him like heat – and he can't blame him. But this is the problem – he reminds himself (another sip): if Adam knows, then Adam can tell – whether on purpose or by mistake. It would have been better if Max hadn't ever met him, hadn't ever visited him, hadn't ever liked him. But he's not a fucking automaton – he's flesh and blood and breathing, and he's allowed to fuck up occasionally, isn't he?

'How is Suraya? And her family? You're very fond of her.'

'She's fine.'

'I'm sure you'd like her to stay that way.'

He tops up the glass. No! No fuck-ups allowed. Not with The Knife poised to strike. From now on he'll keep things tidy. No more meetings with Adam.

There is a prickling behind his eyes. Yes, you cry – like that'll solve every-thing. He lets go of the glass, and then he picks it up and throws it as hard as he can against the wall.

Normally he would've cursed himself for the mess he's made, and quickly, shamefully cleaned it up, erase those glittering specks of anger from the floor. Fuck normally. He ignores the shattered glass. In his bedroom, he peels off his sheepskin slippers and cotton track pants, putting on skinny jeans, black Converse high-tops, a beanie.

In the cab, he squirms when he tells the driver the address – not the name of the club, just its street address. The driver nods knowingly, asks him if he's happy with the radio station (a Christian gospel one) and he insists he is. He wishes he had brought a book to read.

When they pull up outside 15 interminable minutes later, he tips the driver way too much and hastily leaves the vehicle. He sees its taillights trickling up the street as he joins the queue outside Crew and that's when he wonders, with a lurch, what the fuck he's doing.

Because –

Because this is not what he would normally do. Standing outside Crew, drunk, hoping. Hoping for what? Adam? Adam doesn't come to places like this, he can be almost sure of it. Adam is like him, a homebody, a bookworm, a nerd. He should've gone to his flat; no, he couldn't have done that, too risky. So. What is he doing here then? Maybe it isn't Adam, he wonders guiltily. Maybe it was anybody he wanted, or maybe he just wanted to observe them, like he was on one side of an enclosure at the zoo.

So, this is freedom. Volleys of light and sound. The folly. He should not be here. He should be at home, reading. The club is hot, the bodies around him jostle and press. He's in the midst of something churning, obeying its own chaotic, hypnotic logic – a logic he cannot, will not understand. Where is he being carried to, in this dance?

And then he knows.

Before the anger comes, there is the briefest wonderment: why the coin-cidence? Because it is written? And yet it is not – why should it be? There is no Master; there are no puppeteers yanking the strings closer; just fate, just chance – just the slimmest bloody chance that he will see Adam standing close to another man, a beam of light sweeping over them, enveloping them for a second before swishing away.

Yes – it's Adam. Adam so close to a stranger, close enough they might have been kissing; the light didn't linger for long enough to be able to confirm it. Max wants to go walk up to them, wants to push the other man away. Wants to – kiss or punch him. He shudders as something cool, wet slops against his back. He pats his T-shirt, fingers confirming this newfound damp. He sniffs his fingers. Brandy – someone has spilt their brandy on him. He exhales, having almost forgotten he needed to. He slides speedily towards the exit. At the door he looks back to where Adam had been but too many people are in the way to see whether he's still standing there.

'Fuck. Well, babes, you've still got it,' sighs Thabiso as Adam slides out of him, and collapses, shuddering, onto the bed.

In a language more sophisticated than English there is probably a word for this, thinks Adam. A word for having sipped a saucerful of skim milk when what you really wanted was a jumbo milkshake.

Lying on his back, Adam dabs at the cum on his chest with a hand towel. The poppers have left him with a headache. He sighs, pushes himself up, starts pulling on his jeans. Thabiso grabs his forearm.

'Stay the night, babes. I want you to fuck me again in the morning.'

As he rises to standing, Thabiso's hand falls away.

'I can let myself out,' he says.

SUNDAY

[13]

Max pops out to Checkers, buys copies of the *Sunday Times* and *Sunday Press*. Back in his kitchen, he flips through to the latter's culture pages, but there's nothing; no mention of *Vula*, no interview with Adam and Zandile. Has Connie forgotten? It is too soon, he reminds himself; these things take time. He wishes he could send her a reminder, but he knows he can't, The Knife would smell a rat. There is nothing he can do but wait.

His head is tender, throbbing. He wonders if he should call Suraya and suggest lunch, and then, when he is about to ring her, he realises that no, he doesn't want to see her, doesn't want to see anyone except Adam, and he can't, he mustn't, and so he may as well stay here.

MONDAY

[14]

Adam walks along misty Government Avenue. He passes two men in rags sitting on a bench, feeding breadcrumbs to a troop of squirrels. To his right is Tuynhuys, regal and white like a wedding cake, housing the offices of the president of the republic. Hands holding the iron railings separating him from its garden, he stares past the rose bushes to Tuynhuys's windows, wonders if he's imagined the flash of someone inside, looking out.

He lets go of the fence, carries on walking. Now the red brick mass of Parliament looms on his right. CCTV cameras tacked to a colonnade swivel around restlessly. His phone is ringing. It's Zandile.

'Adam! The culture editor at *Sunday Press* rang. She's coming at nine to interview us – about *Vula*. So get that pretty ass of yours to the office.'

TUESDAY

[15]

There is no one, no Max, waiting for Adam when he arrives home. He feels foolish for hoping there would be, for feeling disappointed that there isn't.

Anger like fireworks, a blessed shower of them, blasts away the longing. Fucker! How meagre, those minutes they'd had together – literally just minutes! – at Kirstenbosch.

Poor terrified Max. Would he have stuck around for longer if Adam hadn't mentioned the minister, if he hadn't asked him if he was Richard Lindela's son?

No point in a postmortem. The boy is gone. Good riddance. Troubled Max – way more trouble than all this was worth. Shouldn't be this upset about someone who he barely knows; no, who he doesn't know at all.

In the anger's afterglow he remembers – the holding, the kisses, the warmth. And longing, a glimmer of it, returns.

WEDNESDAY

[16]

The travel agent puts down her gatsby when Max enters Flight Centre, dabbing her mouth with a serviette as he walks up to her counter.

She motions him to sit.

'Thank you. I'd like to fly to London, please.'

'When?'

'Tonight.'

She glances resentfully at her half-eaten lunch, then launches a series of staccato attacks on her keyboard. 'Both of tonight's London flights are full.' More typing, mouse-clicking. 'There's a couple of seats left on the early one tomorrow evening, though?'

His hands are sweating. He wants to beg with her. Tonight. Please. To wait until tomorrow – by then The Knife might have been notified he's been to a travel agent.

'OK,' he sighs. He doesn't trust his voice to issue anything longer than those two syllables.

She tells him the price. He mops his forehead with a coat sleeve. Then, with shaking hands, he unclips his satchel and takes out a wad of cash cinched by an elastic band. Every two or three days he's been withdrawing money in amounts small enough not to arouse suspicion; that way he doesn't have to use his debit card to pay for this – there is no way the transaction can be traced. He counts out the notes, and hands them over to her.

'I hope you're not a drug smuggler, sir,' she says.

THURSDAY

[17]

The subterfuge is as tedious as it is exhausting. Call him snobby, but Max misses the old life right now, the life where going to the airport meant a chauffeured ride at the back of his dad's car. If only. Instead: he rides the train to Salt River Station, then dives onto the platform as the carriage doors begin to judder close. A sprint up and over the tracks to the adjacent taxi rank, hopping into a minibus that is seconds from leaving. Hoping, hoping whoever is following him can't keep up. The minibus taxi weaves between traffic, comes to sudden stops on Main Road to disgorge passengers. The panic in him rises every time they stop. Rises, too, when he hears a siren. He cranes his neck; he manages to make out an ambulance, thank God – it's not the police.

Leaving the minibus at the rank above Cape Town Railway Station, he darts along the pedestrian bridge. He zigzags down side streets, past hawkers and beggars, past workers beginning their wearying journeys home. At last – at last – his feet have brought him to the MyCitiBus terminus at the Civic Centre. An elderly woman follows him onto the airport bus. He sits down in the vehicle's middle; without looking at him, she dodders past him to the rear. He glances back occasionally. She's reading. Still reading. Surely it doesn't take this long to get through the *Cape Argus*? As advertisers and readers have both increasingly abandoned it, the publication has become an emaciated version of its former self – more pamphlet than newspaper. What's taking her so long?

Another look (he can't help himself) as the bus turns off the highway and onto the road approaching the airport. The granny has folded up the *Argus*, is writing on one side of it with a pen. The crossword? Sudoku? Or is she taking notes – does she work for The Knife? It's ridiculous, a little old white lady being one of his spies, but isn't it always those you least suspect, isn't she exactly the kind of person The Knife would use to keep tabs on him?

He closes his eyes. Train, minibus, walk, airport bus. She'd only been there for the final segment. He was being paranoid; he was so close to leaving; it was jitters, just jitters, wasn't it?

*

Check-in, security, immigration. Does the Department of Home Affairs official scanning his passport take longer than usual? Is she reading an alert about him on her computer screen? Her face remains infuriatingly inscrutable as she shoves his passport back under the glass, signals to the next person queuing to come up to her counter.

Max walks away, wet-eyed and dizzy. He sits down near the boarding gate, staring through the window. On the apron, a British Airways Boeing 747 waits, Day-Glo bibbed workers swarming around it like fireflies.

After his boarding pass has been scanned and he is about to enter the air jetty, he sees two policemen stride past, reflected in the glass. They do not spot him. On the plane, he doesn't clip his seatbelt in at first when he sits down. He is still waiting for someone – the policemen, or the granny, or a pair of plainclothes thugs or even The Knife himself to rush down the aisle with pointed fingers. But they don't – no one comes, no one drags him away.

When the jumbo jet takes off, he almost throws up. It feels like they're still on the runway, but they're not – they've lurched and lumbered up into the Cape sky; the airport buildings are already shrinking. The man next to him is praying, a Bible clinging to his protruding stomach.

He is leaving. Jesus Christ. He's leaving!

FRIDAY

[18]

In the passport queue at Heathrow, Max had worried that they would get him then – that somehow the British authorities might have been asked to stop him. But, the man in the turban scanning his passport merely asked him what he was doing in the United Kingdom (holiday) and how long he was staying for (three weeks) and seemed satisfied with the lies that had been told to him.

Now he is here, on the Piccadilly line, watching the ghoul in the glass staring back at him. He closes his eyes. He hardly slept on the flight. The relief has ebbed away: now there is only exhaustion, a desperate urge to lie down. The train rattles out from the dark into pale English morning. The trees are lush; the sky is uncertain, poked at by chimneys and aerials. It is strange – seeing the other passengers, seeing the squiggled map above him, the blue carpeted seats. So strange, so familiar. It is not home but this – London – is still comforting.

Hammersmith. Walking along Shepherds Bush Road and it is like he never left. Changes, sure – but the terraces and the shopfronts seem the same even if some of their names are different. There is a fish and chip shop he doesn't recognise, and the shish kebab place and the Red Cross charity shop and the estate agent. There is the entrance to Tesco's parking lot. Nicolas wine shop. He knows to turn left. A prickling now; he wipes away the tears. Rows of sooty-bricked semi-detached houses. Opposite the school – his old primary school – he stops and opens the gate. He presses the doorbell. It isn't working so he knocks. No reply. He sits down on the mossy steps. He did not expect this – every time he has imagined arriving here, he was not waiting; instead, the door was answered in seconds, and Joan was filling the doorway, surprise turning to joy as she recognised him, as she said, 'Max!'

He doesn't know how long he waits. Maybe it's five minutes – but it's probably more like 20. Joan opens the door. She is wearing a scarf and a trench coat and more wrinkles and tiredness than before. There is a hessian shopping bag in her hand. She looks at him, bewildered.

'Joan. It's Max.'

Only then does she start to smile. 'Max!' Her arms sweep wide and he stoops down to hug her. She smells the same – a powdery, rosy, ancient smell.

When she lets go, and he steps back, she says, 'Well, this is a lovely surprise. What are you doing in London? Come now, let's get you inside.'

In the kitchen, she fills up the kettle and puts it on the Aga.

'I'm sorry for just turning up,' he says. 'I lost your email address; I had some trouble with my account and everything got deleted two months ago.'

She reaches up, selects two cups – willow patterned ones she only ever used for special occasions, he remembers – and places them on a tray.

'Not a problem. Golly. It's wondreous to see you. You've grown up so beautifully. You're a proper gentleman.'

'I was wondering if I could stay – just for a few days. I'm going backpacking in the Lake District next week.'

'Of course you can,' she beams.

While Joan is grocery shopping, Max drinks a second cup of tea. He sits at the small table, ensconced in the familiar, in the faded, shiny warmth. He gazes out at the yard. The once-taut washing line droops over a lawn that has become choked with weeds.

Joan has shown him the spare bedroom in the attic. Nothing of his is left, not even the bed. Instead, a sofa. She has pulled down two pillows and a blanket. He arranges these to his liking, and falls asleep.

The old white lady is on the bus again, on today's double-decker. He looks at her again. She is wearing sunglasses and a felt hat (not the outfit she had in Cape Town), but it must be her; he is sure of it. He shivers. He wants to get off. He wants to press the STOP button, but he doesn't. He watches a baby in its pram and the glower clouding its face. Outside, sun flickers across windows. He waits and he breathes. The old white lady remains – she does not get off when the mother with the pram does. He waits and then, when the Palace Gate stop is announced, he hops off. He watches the bus trundle away. He walks into Kensington Gardens. He wants to run, but he forces himself not to. She cannot follow him now. And here he is safe. He shouldn't have taken the bus. He should've walked to the internet café. Whatever. He is here now, walking slowly round the pond, watching the swans.

The sun is flailing – caught by drifting clouds. The water glints – mercury, pewter, an alternate sheen. He will walk to the trees, he's decided. He will follow the thinnest path until the traffic fades and only a runner's footsteps sound. He has sat down. It is dry; the grass is almost dusty. His hands feel the pressure of the earth pushing upwards; he is slightly dizzy; his head fizzes backwards, gently touching the grass.

The leaves blanket him. He does not sleep – the coffee he had earlier has banished tiredness. But here is dreaming of some kind – is it imagined, this waking, and Adam next to him, and for silent minutes they just hold each other and breathe?

He stands up too fast. Swaying, he has to grab the trunk to stop himself from falling back down.

The new *Vula* story – the one about gold smuggling in Zimbabwe that Adam posted on the site yesterday – has already been shared and liked by more people on Facebook than "The President" has been in over a week. Adam does not tell Zandile this; he has decided to keep his disappointment to himself. The *Sunday Press* article might help; but there are no guarantees the piece will even run. No one cares about gay presidents, about gay rights – not even the gays do: there was barely a whimper of protest after Richard Lindela's speech. Max, Zandile, Adam – the three of them have failed.

Max is dreaming again – a too-familiar dream. His dad is leaning forward, elbows on his desk, fingers pointing: an arrow to the chandelier. Max says it, finally: *I am gay.* His dad stares at him. Max closes his eyes and waits. His dad clears his throat. There is no fierceness, just frightening calm. He is saying – *This is not what I fought for. I did not suffer so you could choose this life.*

Max replies: *I didn't choose it – I would never have chosen it! – it's just the way I am.*

His dad snorts: *Of course you chose this. You have shown contempt for all we have sacrificed. Your mother – think of her now.*

His dad is talking so softly that Max can scarcely hear him. *You do not deserve the freedom we fought for, the freedom your mother died for*, he says. He stands up, walks to the open door; he disappears.

Max stands up too. He goes to the door, to the long corridor. His dad has gone. And then the soldiers come, they tug him through an archway, to a quadrangle. His feet drag on the gravel as they pull him – he can hear the long scratches, the final beating: his heart or a drum. They let go of him. He collapses against the wall. He stands up slowly, edges back against it. He looks up to the roof where his dad is standing, flanked by the president and The Knife. The soldiers raise their rifles. Safety catches click in unison. He waits.

SATURDAY

[19]

Max has left Joan, uncomplaining Joan, to catch up on *Strictly*. They have hardly talked – there seems surprisingly little to say – or little that can be said. There is plenty that can't be. Returning now, after all this time, has stirred up questions he had never wondered before. How did they find her, this retired English nurse? How much did they pay her? And why did they choose her instead of an exile – instead of someone from home? There must have been plenty in London, after all.

He has walked past the Tube station, past the church, under the flyover and onwards to the Thames. He stops halfway across Hammersmith Bridge, looks at the grey, flecked with silver. He can see it too easily: the quick clamber, the bent knees, the arms floating, the fall, the blessed fall. He holds the metal tight. The cars are louder now. His fingers loosen. He begins walking again. He reaches the other end. He has not jumped.

Down the steps onto the footpath, into the shadowed green. Leaves curtain the water. Two runners pound past, luminous and sweaty. And then stillness again: the city has shrunk back; the plants have triumphed. And here, not quite remembering, just thinking of the green tapestry above, seeing no sky, just feeling the flashes of sun as Joan pushed his pram.

He stops. There is an opening; the river is framed by branches. Rowers fight the water like knives on refrigerated butter. The coxswain is shouting. He looks back towards the bridge. There is a figure in the distance; too far away to identify. Max starts walking again, faster now. He looks behind. The speck is getting closer. Should he wait in the bushes? Should he hide?

In Bloomsbury. He is alive – still! His followers haven't murdered him yet; maybe they're only keeping tabs on him (or maybe they don't exist). He leans against iron railings. Bright bodies flow past him towards the solemnity of the British Museum. He remembers – only vaguely – his single visit here when he was seven or eight. His father marched him from room to room, a finger jabbing towards the masks and pots and jewellery entombed in glass. Hissing: Stolen. Looted, these treasures. Taken from us. His tone seemed to suggest

Max was at least partly responsible for the desecration. Max was trying not to cry. It wasn't me; I didn't do it. And then, the urgent, unbearable question: When you go, can I come with you? We can bring all this back? But he hadn't said a word. Instead he had looked at each plaque and nodded and prayed.

He is not a tourist; he will not go in today. Instead he walks on, heading down Bury Place to the London Review Bookshop. Amongst the shelves, he scans the spines, pulls books out, replaces them. He feels again a question – but it is unarticulated, just a feeling, an urge, a disturbance that makes his eyes gloss across the text as he flips through pages. He puts down the book he is holding, leaves the shop.

He joins the choke of commuters entering Holborn Tube station. He gets on a train, eyes closing as it clatters eastwards, opening when the St Paul's stop is announcement. Up, up to the City's Saturday emptiness. There are people, of course, in front of the Cathedral. They sit on the steps licking ice creams, taking selfies. He crosses the road, walks towards the river. The Millennium Bridge is right in front of him, curving up beyond an accordion player. He continues past him onto the bridge and looks back. There it is – the building. Dark glass conceals its innards. A Canadian flag flaps diffidently at its front.

It is the writer's curse: that urge to know the reasons why; what motivates himself, and others – why do we do what we do? And it grates Max, this surely illogical impulse – he would never write a character doing this: he cannot tell why, yet again, he is on the Tube, and why he is then walking through the warm evening from Old Street and why he is in the George & Dragon ordering a glass of wine.

He stands near a gold pillar. His eyes dart up to the disco ball and the stuffed parakeet and fake flamingo, then bounce against the disco ball, sliding above the bar's bottles, bottles studded with plastic fruit. He blinks. A short, stocky mustachioed man is sidling up to him, asking him if he wants to join him and his mates. He jabs a thumb in their direction. They leer in a corner booth; they are watching, waiting for his reaction.

'No thank you,' he says. The rebuff must have sounded harsher than he intended because the man replies – 'Well, I'm sorry for having disturbed you; you looked lonely, that's all.' He twirls around and steps back to his friends.

Max goes to the bar for more wine; squeezes between two biggish men. He can almost feel a hand on his butt while he's ordering, but when he looks around there is nothing and he knows – it is just this place; it makes his skin itch. He feels terrible for feeling that. Surely – this pub is an oasis, a victory. He pays and steps back into the room. He goes outside where deepening blue ekes through thick leaves; drinkers cluster, some look at him admiringly and there is a spark of something in him at this attention; it warms him, for once, instead of scaring him. He goes back inside for another glass; he knows he is being reckless but he doesn't care. He is on autopilot, he's decided – who cares if it will crash him? But instead of wine he has a double whisky and is reminded of that first night with Adam, darling Adam. Why can't he be here now – why can't he be here in London? He takes a sip, but it does not quench the aching.

SUNDAY

[20]

Adam is sitting at the deli round the corner from his flat, the newspaper folded out in front of him.

Zandile answers him on the second ring.

'Have you seen it?' she asks.

'Yes, I've got it here. It's a news story – page four. I don't get it; I thought it was going to be in the culture section. All she's written about is "The President". Not about anything else we've published.'

'Clearly that's her angle. But don't sound so disappointed. We're in the news! This story is going to get the attention it deserves. We should be grateful it wasn't some long-winded feature at the back of the paper.'

Adam puts the phone down. Something is churning in his stomach – it is coffee, or excitement, or fear.

Max buys an iPad from the Apple Store on Regent Street. It has put a huge dent in his savings but he doesn't care; what use are those funds sitting in his account? He uses the store's free wifi to check *Sunday Press*'s website. Near the top of the page, there's a headline and subheading that makes his heart start galloping.

The gay president and other stories

A cheeky online journal is shaking up local literature

At long fucking last! He clicks on the story. Scrolls past the portrait of Adam and Zandile leaning nonchalantly against the railings in front of Parliament.

He begins reading.

Little more than a year since its launch, the online literary journal *Vula* is already making a stir. Last week it published a provocative short story in which an African country's president has sex with a rent boy. The raunchy story does not mention the country in which it is set.

Vula, which publishes a short story every Thursday, was created by Lekgotla, a small branding agency, "to provide a platform for great writing and important ideas".

"We're passionate about quality, vibrant writing, particularly stories which provoke, challenge and question," says Adam Miller, its editor.

When asked about the background to the new story, Miller was tight-lipped, admitting that "Gabriel Roberts" was a pseudonym. "Given the recent developments around LGBT rights in this country and elsewhere, we thought it an apt piece to publish at this time. But, perhaps understandably, the person who wrote this piece did not feel comfortable publishing it in their own name."

The provocative story was published a day after Richard Lindela, the Minister of Traditional Affairs, called for a commission to explore the legality of same-sex relations, describing homosexuals as "a decadent minority with un-African values who seek to corrupt our communities with their unnatural tendencies".

"This story is not an attack on our nation's president," said *Vula*'s co-founder Zandile Sithole. "It is a cheeky attempt to encourage empathy amongst people of all sexualities, to promote tolerance of diversity, and to question assumptions around patriarchal heteronormativity."

The president's official spokesman was unavailable for comment. When approached for comment, Minister Lindela's spokesman, Tommy Seko, said that although he hadn't heard of *Vula* before, the news that such a story had been published was "deeply dismaying". "We must still investigate this, but certainly if what you are saying is correct then, at this stage, we are concerned that the dignity of the president has been impinged upon. We should never confuse the sacrosanct right to the freedom of expression with insulting others."

Seko said that the ministry would be releasing a fuller statement soon. When asked for comment, Steven Hambly, the executive vice-president of the South African Society for Literature said, "It's not really for us to comment on the nature of the short story, or its literary merit. But we do welcome the vibrancy of literary engagement that is emerging in the digital space which clearly *Vula* forms a part of. It is only through the nation being in conversation with itself that this country can truly move forward, interrogating and exploring our progress as it does so."

Vusi Sese, CEO of Arts-Nation, the state-funded body which aims to increase access to the arts and provides grants to writers and artists, was less complimentary. "We are at the front and centre of encouraging creative expression. Writing is an important tool to give voice to the people, a voice that was quashed for so long. But it should be used for healing, to build our nation up, not as a tool for slander."

READ THE SHORT STORY ONLINE AT READVULA.COM/THEPRESIDENT

Max clicks on the link which takes him to the story. There are now more than 300 comments trailing beneath it.

OUR PREZ ISNT GAY

BULLSHIT! THIS IS LIES.

WHY ARE THE GAYS ALLEGING THIS?
THEY WANT EVERYONE TO BE GAY

And, right at the very bottom:

GABRIEL ROBERTS MUST DIE!

Max closes the browser window, deletes the past hour's browsing history. Everything is different now – not because of the death threat (which he feels oddly detached from). The newspaper, it's in the newspaper: now the spark has flared. Where will the wind take it?

MONDAY

[21]

Adam's phone has vibrated in his pocket and so, before he crosses the road with his bike, he fishes it out. A text message from Lindiwe: Have you seen the papers? P.S. Pls come over for dinner this eve with Zandile at 6.30pm. He could read them online, but he'd rather pursue them in print, and so he goes to the 7-Eleven and picks up four morning dailies. Each of them have articles quoting from the statement Richard Lindela has released. In the office, while the kettle boils, he scans through them. They pretty much say the same thing. Here, for example, on page three of *Business Day*:

Minister slams 'gay president' story

Sipho Sigcau, Political Reporter

CAPE TOWN—The Minister of Traditional Affairs, Richard Lindela, has slammed the publication of "The President", a sexually explicit short story which features, he claims, the president of this country. The piece was published last week in the online literary journal *Vula* (readvula.com) a day after Lindela announced in the National Assembly that he wanted to set up a commission investigating whether the rights of gay people should remain constitutionally enshrined.

"This disgusting story provides even more proof that the gay agenda is committed to demeaning the dignity of our culture, our president, and our democracy. It is offers proof that we need to take action against this scourge," he said in a statement released last night. He described the story as "an assault on our values, masquerading behind the fig leaf of artistic expression".

"The gay white bourgeoisie is determined to corrupt our people, and while doing so, insult and belittle those who sacrificed so much in our fight for freedom. Our freedom is under attack. When such contempt is shown for the dignity we fought so hard for, it is clear that our freedom is theoretical, not real. Until there is respect for our culture, and for our democratically elected leaders, we remain oppressed."

"This government is committed to protecting the right to freedom of expression. But we believe this cannot trump the right our president and his people have to dignity," Lindela said. He believed the use of a pseudonym illustrated "cowardice and weakness" he alleged was typical of this "decadent minority". The minister stated he will make representations to the publisher, requesting that the story is removed from the website. If it refuses to comply, unspecified "further action" will be taken.

Adam's phone is ringing – a call from a unknown number. He answers.

'Is this Adam Miller?'

'This is he.'

'I'm Veronique Martins, the producer for Sheryl Tshwete's afternoon talk show on SAfm. Would you be happy to come into the studio to talk about the gay president story later?'

Do I have to? He wonders.

'OK,' he replies.

'Can't we both do the interview?'

'No, Ad, you'll be fine.' Zandile rummages in her bag. 'Just take some of this Rescue Remedy beforehand.'

He is nauseous. He has looked at the stats – thousands of people read the story yesterday, and this morning. Hundreds have left comments below the story. He turns to Zandile. 'I didn't realise people would be quite so awful – have you seen some of these comments?'

Zandile turns to face him.

'Ad! Stop reading those now. Ignore the trolls, it's really not worth thinking about. You'll only scare yourself.'

He does not tell her that some of them mention her. Some of them call her 'traitor', 'self-hating fat bitch', 'coconut whore'. He hadn't been expecting this anger, this fiercely vindictive vitriol – against him, her, 'Gabriel Roberts'.

He closes the tab. 'To be honest, Zands, I am a little bit scared.'

'It's our 15 minutes of fame, hon; it'll blow over soon. Don't be scared; enjoy the attention while it lasts.'

His phone is ringing again. Another blocked number.

'Hello, are you Adam Miller?' A woman's voice, bored.

'Yes.'

'I've got Minister Richard Lindela on the line for you. Please hold one second.' There's a pause and then –

'Adam, how are you?'

He is a little surprised by the cheeriness of the greeting.

'Morning, minister. I'm well, thanks. And you?'

'I've had better days to be honest. Now. As you would've seen, we've had a look at this website of yours.' Adam does not say anything and so the minister continues. 'This kind of insult to the president is completely unacceptable.'

'It's fiction, sir. Just a story.'

'But it utterly demeans him. It's disgraceful.' The voice is less cheery now.

'That's your opinion, Minister, and you're entitled to it.'

'It needs to be removed.'

Adam swallows. He can almost hear his heartbeat. 'That isn't going to happen.'

'We would like it to be removed and to find out who wrote it.'

'I can't tell you that either, sir.'

'Well, young Adam, I'm very sorry to hear that. But we'll give you a little bit of time to reconsider. You have until Thursday to remove it, or we'll take action.'

The line goes dead. Adam puts the phone down. He looks at his hands. They're shaking.

Max watches the rain trickling down the window. He has seen on *Vula*'s Twitter feed that Adam will be speaking on SAfm. His iPad sits in his lap; the radio station's website is already loaded. At noon GMT, he presses its livestream button.

Crackling through his headphones, he hears: '... the editor of *Vula*. Hello, Adam.'

'Hello Sheryl, how are you?'

Eyes closes. It's Adam's voice. Far away, a little disembodied, but unmistakably Adam.

'Well, thank you. Now Adam, as I've been explaining to our listeners, a short story you've published seems to have caused quite a fuss. How do you respond to Minister Richard Lindela's call to remove "The President" from *Vula*?'

'We won't be taking the story down. The minister and, indeed, the president, will just have to get used to that.'

'Did you publish this because you think it's a great story? Or is it simply intended to irritate and offend powerful people, Adam?'

There's a slight pause. 'It's definitely a great story – we wouldn't have published it if it wasn't. But a major reason for us publishing it is to encourage people to think about sexuality, to question their entrenched assumptions, to foster greater tolerance.'

'But is that really what you're doing by being so controversial? After all, the minister is claiming that the story provides proof that gay people are committed to – and I quote – 'demeaning the dignity of our culture, our president, our democracy'. He's also alleging that gays are trying 'to corrupt our people'. How would you respond to that?'

'I think the minister is being hysterical. This is a short story. The gays of this country aren't forcing anyone to read it. And his belief that it is demeaning is his interpretation of the story, and not necessarily the writer's intent.'

'Clearly publishing this is a reaction of sorts to the Minister's announcement last week that he wants gay rights to be reviewed.'

'It was certainly the right time to publish it, yes. The minister claims that gays are determined to convert everyone. But there's no proof of this. He's just using gay people as a scapegoat – a useful distraction to take our minds off the Congress's broken promises and rampant corruption.'

'Adam, did you write this? Are you gay?'

'I am gay, yes. But no, I didn't write it.'

'Who did?'

'I can't answer that. The writer deliberately chose a pseudonym.'

'Isn't that a bit cowardly?'

'Hardly. I think it's perfectly understandable given the levels of prejudice against gays in this country. Have you seen the comments below the piece? There are people calling for Gabriel Roberts to be killed.'

'That's shocking. Why are you allowing those comments to be published?'

'Because I'm less fond of censorship than Minister Lindela is. His claim that this story is an attack on freedom is rather ironic considering that the ones attacking freedom right now are the ruling party acolytes who are leaving such vicious comments at the bottom of the story. If the minister is so concerned about the state of democracy, he should be fostering a plurality of voices and identities – including those he disagrees with.'

'Even if they insult his leader?'

'Absolutely. Each of us has the right to insult each other. The Minister is most welcome to call me names. Unlike some, I can take it on the chin. Though I must stress – there's nothing particularly insulting about this short story. There's nothing wrong with a gay president.'

'Thanks, Adam. Now if you can just hold on the line, we're going to take some calls... Right, hello, we have Thembi from Emalahleni – '

'*Sjoe*! I am revolted by this man, Sheryl. How can you let this filth on your show? This man? He is trying to corrupt us.'

'How?' replies Sheryl. 'As he pointed out, you didn't have to read the story.'

'This man, this Adam. You are trying to impose yourself and your tendencies on us. You think you whites know better, that you can put your penis inside the Black anus. But we – '

'Thanks Thembi, I think we get the picture,' Sheryl says. 'Now, we have Nomsa on the line from Durban. Hello?'

'Hello Sheryl. I am a Black woman.'

'Black like me, hey?'

'Yes, Sheryl. And I want to tell you all this is ridiculous. The minister thinks only white people and the people they allegedly convert are gays. That is nonsense. Let me tell you about my son. He grew up on the farm. There were no whites around. And his best friend in school – they were lovers. And then they go to the city, to university and – '

'Thank you,' Sheryl says.

'I think we should listen to the rest of her story, Sheryl,' Adam says. 'Nomsa's making an important point. There are gays of every colour.'

'We really do need to wrap it up, now. Adam Miller, thank you for joining us.'

Max removes his headphones. He wishes he could call Adam. He wants to congratulate him, warn him. But he cannot.

Adam checks his phone as he leaves the radio studio. Eleven missed calls – either from blocked numbers or ones he doesn't recognise. Who the fuck are these people? The media? How did they get his number?

OMG you're famous! xx, says a text from Jaco. There is another message, from Zandi: The Rescue Remedy worked! You were brilliant!

He won't tell her that before he went into the interview he'd had two shots of vodka at the bar down the road. He wonders what he said earlier; what did he say when he was sitting in front of the microphone? All he remembers is the anger; somehow the anger turned into the words that firmly, calmly left his mouth.

Now he is watching the sea, holding the railings, wishing he could have another drink. His phone is vibrating. It's his dad. He wonders if he should ignore it. He picks up.

'What the fuck are you doing, Adam? Are you out of your mind?'

'Dad – '

'I really don't give a damn about you being gay. But do you have to rub it in everyone's faces?'

'Dad – '

'This isn't Europe, my boy. Show some respect. These people's culture – it's different. You really shouldn't have published that story; it's clearly pissed them off.'

'It's a free country, Dad. Anyone should be able to say what they want.'

'It's their country, Adam. Don't you get it? This is the new South Africa. Times have changed. You want to live here, you play by their rules.'

'I don't think that's quite what the constitution says. In fact, the constitution contains the only rules we should be playing by and they apply to all South Africans, of every race.'

'I really hope you grow up fast, Adam. You're playing with fire. And I hope to God they don't find out that you and I are related. The bank does a lot of business with the party; I deal with these guys all the time. I would hate them to think I share your disrespect for their culture and their president.'

'Sorry, Dad, I've got to go – I've got another call coming.'

He switches his phone off. He does not want to talk to anyone else now. Already, before the interview, he had been asked for comment by how many – five? – newspapers, and gave a soundbite to another radio station. He has said the same things over and over again, and still they want more.

Max wakes up. It's 4pm. He had fallen asleep on the couch. The iPad wakes up after charging for several excruciating minutes.

He Googles: gay president gabriel roberts vula.

The same wire story is up on several news websites. On NewsLine, its headline is Minister threatens court action against 'gay president' story. A new media statement is being quoted from:

Minister Richard Lindela takes note of the public refusal made earlier today by the editor of *Vula* to remove the offensive and demeaning story. In the spirit of tolerance, the minister has decided to give this website until 12pm on Thursday to remove the offensive piece. Should this not occur, legal proceedings will commence to restore dignity to the president.

Max checks Twitter. #therealGabrielRoberts is trending.

LET US HUNT DOWN THE #THEREALGABRIELROBERTS
#THEREALGABRIELROBERTS MUST DIE

WHEN WE FIND #THEREALGABRIELROBERTS LET US RIP OPEN
HIS ANUS – OH WAIT, HE WILL ENJOY THAT, LET'S JUST
SHOOT HIM.

FAGS LIKE #THEREALGABRIELROBERTS ARE EVIL. WE SHOULD
TAKE CARE OF THEM ALL!

#THEREALGABRIELROBERTS IS A PRETTY COURAGEOUS MOFO.
STOP HATING

#THEREALGABRIELROBERTS MUST STOP LYING. WE WILL TEACH
HIM THE TRUTH ABOUT OUR PRESIDENT.

THE PRESIDENT ISN'T GAY, #THEREALGABRIELROBERTS,
U JUST WISH HE WAS U SICK BASTARD.

GAYS LIKE #THEREALGABRIELROBERTS SHOULD DIG THEIR OWN
GRAVE BEFORE WE SHOOT THEM.

TOO BAD #THEREALGABRIELROBERTS ISN'T A REAL MAN

#THEREALGABRIELROBERTS IS A COWARD. COME OUT,

SHOW YOUR FACE!

US PATRIOTS WILL FIND #THEREALGABRIELROBERTS...
YOU CANNOT ESCAPE, YOU WILL SUFFER

#THEREALGABRIELROBERTS HATES BLACK PEOPLE

#THEREALGABRIELROBERTS YOU MIGHT LIKE FUCKING,
BUT YOU'LL NEVER FORGET A PITCHFORK THROUGH
YOUR BUMHOLE

FUCKING HELL. I TOTALLY UNDERSTAND WHY
#THEREALGABRIELROBERTS PUBLISHED UNDER A PSEUDONYM.

#THEREALGABRIELROBERTS BETTER BE FAR AWAY,
FOR HIS OWN SAKE

THE BIGGEST PROBLEM WITH FINDING
#THEREALGABRIELROBERTS IS THAT WE ONLY GET A CHANCE
TO KILL HIM ONCE.

#THEREALGABRIELROBERTS YOU DESERVE TO DIE.

I'LL MOER #THEREALGABRIELROBERTS WITH MY OWN HANDS.
LET'S FIGHT 4 FREEDOM, LET'S HUNT HIM DOWN

THIS #THEREALGABRIELROBERTS SHIT IS SCARY.
#ITSSCARYTOBEGAYOK

Nauseous and trembling, he puts down the iPad and closes his eyes. At tea-time, he and Joan sit down for some ham and pea soup. The salty liquid is scalding but he sips it anyway. She asks him if he's OK, and he just nods. She purses her lips, clearly dubious, but does not press him.

On the South Bank, Max leans over the railings, spots a solitary plane leaf drifting downstream. The smell of roasting peanuts – or the jangle of nerves inside him – is making him want to retch. What is he doing here, there are too many people – too many people queuing for the Eye, wandering towards the National Theatre, watching mimes and breakdancers and skateboarders. He is still trying not to think about it, trying to look at the Thames, but still the fear holds him. What is next? What would he say to Adam if he could? If he could call him now? Something inside him lurches, tearing away from him like a kite in the wind. The backlash was inevitable. He knows this, had always known this. Is it fair on them, though – on Adam and Zandi? Still. They had chosen his story – he hadn't forced them to publish it: they had made the choice to. Yet that's hardly consolation for what they face now. And, worse, he is not there to face it with them.

He hears Joan coming slowly up the stairs; she appears with a cup of tea. He thanks her, puts the book he's been reading down. He decided – he will ask.
'Joan...'
'Yes?'
His tongue feels heavy as it tries to excavate the words he needs. 'After Mom died, why didn't I live with my dad? Why did he send me here, to London?'
'Your father was worried about what could happen to you. Thought you'd be safer here – safer in Europe than on the African continent. Though poor Dulcie still got murdered – in Paris, of all places – so I s'pose nowhere was truly safe, was it?'
Max nods. 'And... why... after... after the elections, the first democratic ones – '94 – when everyone went home, everyone else... why did I stay in London? Why didn't my father bring me back?'
'He thought it would be less disruptive for you to finish your primary schooling here.'
He nods.
'I know he didn't visit often, but he did love and care about you.'
He nods, gripping his book tightly, blinking furiously. She can tell he doesn't believe her, can't she?

As she hands Adam a glass of red wine, Lindiwe declares she's incredibly proud of him and Zandile.
'Hold fast, you two. This could end up being quite ugly, but you can't let those bastards bully you into submission. So much is riding on this. You've got to stand up for what's right. We've got to prove the Struggle was not in vain. That human rights, freedom of expression, still count for something. That this

truly is a *new* South Africa – not bigoted and repressive like the old one.'

'Cheers to that. Censorship is *so* '80s,' says Zandile, raising her glass.

Adam envies their unruffled certitude.

His mother phones him as they are tucking into dessert. He wouldn't have answered if it had been someone else, but it's his mom, and so, apologising, he wriggles out of his chair and goes into the living room to take her call.

'Adam-pie, is everything OK?'

'Fine, everything is peachy,' he tells her carefully, hoping he isn't slurring – he must've drunk at least a bottle's worth of Cab Sauv by now.

'*Vula* was on the TV news this evening. The ruling party seems extremely upset with that story you've published.'

'Yes, they are.'

'What are you going to do?'

'We're not removing it.'

There is a pause. 'That's my boy. I am so proud of you. The minister can't dictate to you what you can publish and can't. Imagine if they told me what kind of ceramics I could make!'

'Well, just don't make any sculptures that look like the president,' he tells her. They both laugh. He is quiet during the rest of the dinner. Lindiwe's strident tones wash over him. He barely notices Zandi's glances, barely responds when she asks if he's OK.

He wants to be alone. He doesn't want to be right. He wants to be alone, and away from all this. They are in the papers, on radio and the web; they are being beamed into lounges on TV sets. Is this really what they signed up for? How much longer are they going to have to put up with this?

He wonders if Max knew this would happen. Surely? That must be why he went away. Is this what he wanted? Why? He must be Lindela's son – or someone else's son. He wanted to be Samson, but the story hadn't brought the edifice down on the ruling party. It was him – Adam – who was becoming engulfed. Him and Zandile. And 'Gabriel Roberts'. Where the fuck is Max? Adam imagines him lying in a hammock next to a turquoise sea, smoking a joint, smiling lazily. Hatred, or something similarly hot, burns in him. As he stacks the dirty plates in Lindiwe's dishwasher, he remembers that night – it feels like aeons ago now – when they stood together in the dark, when Max had been so loving, so soft, ushering him gently to bed. The hatred has gone, he notices; something else has replaced it. Love. Or maybe just longing.

A wish they'd had more time, more encounters, more togetherness.

As Lindiwe hugs them goodbye she says, 'I'm here for you.' She squeezes Adam tightly. 'Keep fighting.'

Maybe she knows. Knows that Adam is – well, not wavering, but perhaps a little resentful. Maybe the *Why me? Why us?* is written on his face. Or maybe she just knows what it is like to face the fury of those in power. She never talks about those years – fleeing from policemen's bullets to Swaziland when she was still just a teen. But he realises that it is there, that time – etched into her, unforgotten.

He isn't alone. He must remember that – there is Zandile and Lindiwe. There must be others too. He wonders if he should call Thabiso. Would it make a difference if the Official Opposition released a statement supporting them? Would it make it worse?

Zandile drops him off at his flat. In his own bed, he lurches into sleep, into a dream, where there is someone, maybe Max, maybe Raees, maybe even Thabiso, next to him, holding him, watching him sleep.

TUESDAY

[22]

Adam wakes up early, too early. His head hurts. He can't face running on the mountain, so instead he takes his bike out. He whizzes down through the quiet dark towards the ocean. Mist muffles the water's lazy rumbling. On the Sea Point Promenade there are one or two joggers, ghosts gathering definition as he speeds passed them. He reaches stairs down to a small beach and dismounts, carrying the bike onto the sand. He takes off his shoes and socks, and runs towards the water. A wave comes, swallowing his ankles, so cold his feet ache.

He gets to the office before eight. He's grateful he has a full, uninterrupted morning ahead of him: the radio interview swallowed up too much time yesterday, and there are deadlines he has to deliver on today.

As he unlocks the door, he stops – a smell, a foul faecal smell, is flooding his nostrils. He wonders if a homeless person has shat nearby, and then he looks up at the brown smears on the shopfront next to the entrance. He blinks. The smears form letters and the letters say:

EVIL GAYS !

They know – whoever did this knows the office is here, well, on the second floor. At the moment the ground floor is empty; a café was once here, and now it is just an empty space, with **TO LET** signs tacked to the glass.

He is relieved at this – that is what he thinks first: relief that he doesn't have to apologise to the grouchy Greek who used to run the place until it shuttered.

He takes his bike inside and shuts the door, making sure it's locked behind him.

The three letters are spread out on his desk. The first is printed out (in Calibri font – 'how unoriginal' – sniffs Zandile).

VULA MAGAZIN
DO NOT DESRISPECT OUR PRECEDENT!
YOU WILL PAY 4 THIS.

The second is handwritten.

Dear Gabriel Roberts
You piece of faggot shit. You're worth nothing, moffie trash.
You deserve to die.
Be <u>very</u>, <u>very</u> careful.

The third uses letters cut out from magazines like a ransom note in the movies.

MOFFiE^s
wE
R   C0 mi*n* g

F°R *u*

Adam's face has gone white; his palms are clammy. 'How do people know our offices are here? Our address isn't publicly listed anywhere, is it?'

Zandile shrugs. 'People have their ways and means.'

'I think we should take these to the police.'

'That's the done thing, yes. Not that it'll make a stitch of difference.'

Adam's phone is ringing. It is from an unknown number, but he decides he better answer it anyway.

'Adam speaking,' he mutters, eyes and mind still on the press release in front of him he's been proofreading.

Silence. He puts his pen down. 'Hel-lo?'

Still nothing. He puts the phone down.

'Who was that?'

'I don't know. They didn't say anything. Not a word.' Adam coughs, trying to banish the panic that's beginning to grip his oesophagus. 'Do you think we're in real danger?'

Zandile swivels round in her chair to face him, shaking her head. 'It's just intimidation. No one really wants to kill us. It's a piddly little short story, for God's sake. They're hoping we'll get frightened and take it down. Classic bully move.'

'What makes you so sure we're not at risk? What if the people who wrote those things really mean it?'

Zandile gets up and puts her arms around him. 'Sit tight, Ad. It'll be fine.'

Max sits with his iPad in his lap, watching a clip of the Congress Youth League's media conference, which has just been posted on the state broadcaster's website. The camera zooms in on the League's corpulent leader who is sitting behind a thicket of microphones. The man clears his throat, glances down at some notes, looks up, furious, at the seated journalists.

'Our oppressors are attacking us – the fight for freedom is far from over,' he splutters. 'These whites. These gay whites are hijacking our democracy for their own nefarious ends. They are determined to belittle our great leader. They say he is gay too. They are lying! Our president – the president of the Congress and of the Republic of South Africa – is a mighty man, the manliest man among many. And he has many wives. We must fight these lies. We must fight for dignity. We must fight against the scourge of these sick monsters who wish to enslave us with their decadent deceit.' He lifts a finger. 'I say to you – I say, 'Watch it.' We will fight. We will find out who this Gabriel Roberts is. We will find him and we will teach him about freedom. We will teach him. We will march to the offices of this evil publication, this so-called *Vula*, this most racist place. We will bring the democratic revolution there. We will set the people free.' He stands up now. His voice is just softer than a shout. 'We will defend our democracy against foreign forces! We will protect our children from evil! We will fight against the racism and oppression which lives on! Aluta continua – the struggle continues!'

Joan appears at the top of the stairs. 'Your father called,' she says.

Max almost drops the iPad. He looks at her smile, and looks away, at the embroidered picture on the wall: a stone farmhouse against plump green hills.

'He was just calling to find out how I was.'

Max nods, forces his eyes to meet hers. That's not remotely suspicious, is it? Out of the blue, the busy, busy cabinet minister finding time to call the woman who used look after his son – who hasn't been responsible for him for well over a decade. A courtesy call... merely to find out how she is? No, not suspicious at all.

'Max, he didn't know you were in London. He didn't know you were staying with me.' He wipes his hands on the blanket, stares at the blank screen in his lap. He swallows the spit pooling in his mouth. Then he stares at her for long enough to make her look away. He is sinking now. He hasn't thought it through, properly, damnit. He hasn't thought about The Knife. He'd been so relieved to get on that plane, to get to London, to get to Joan. But The Knife must have been wondering – the silence, why the silence? If he hadn't spotted it already, a quick enquiry would've shown it: the record showing his departure. It would be on a Department of Home Affairs server surely – his name and passport number and the date he left the country. Easy. And now – he would've figured it out: Joan. But then – what would The Knife have told his father? *Your son has fled the country. He's staying with that old git Joan Fletcher who used to look after him.* Surely not – because his dad would be wondering why his son was being monitored. Could this call just be a coincidence?

His head is hurting. What should he say? Their eyes have met again.

'He said he wondered why he couldn't get hold of you. He said he would call tomorrow to chat. Is that OK?'

There is a second when he wonders if he should fight it: the trembling, flickering moment when composure might be still salvageable. But it is not: he is crying now; he is shaking. Joan steps forward softly, sits down on the sofa next to him. She takes his left hand and holds it.

'Max, we always knew not to ask questions. We had to just accept the mysteries of comings and goings; we had to. But that was then; this is now. The Struggle is over.'

Max coughs. He wants to ask her – are you sure you know nothing? What did my Dad really say? But he daren't ask this. He can see the hares flailing in the headlights. They don't get away. He can't get away. He's hopping now, in his head, wishing he could turn to the darkness, unable to. What is next?

'I'm sorry,' he says eventually. 'I didn't want him to know. I was worried he would be angry. You see: I'm bunking my classes to travel here. I needed a break. I'm struggling to fit in at university. I don't have any friends.

I thought if I went away for a few weeks... went hiking... was in a different, a completely different place....'

She nods. 'You poor boy,' she says, squeezing his hand.

He hears the thumps of his feet on the steep carpeted stairs as if they're duetting with his heartbeat. If he goes any faster, he will fall. The door shuts behind him and he is outside, and running, wondering if Joan is watching him from the window, wondering if she's phoning someone – his dad? The Knife? His head swirls around looking for signs of anything suspicious.

At Shepherds Bush Road he stops. Only a few more days, almost there. This is Europe – he's not in Cape Town anymore. He'll be fine. Or will he?

As Joan has reminded him, Europe hadn't been faraway enough to spare his mom's friend, Dulcie. The Congress's representative to France and Luxembourg. Gunned down at her office by unknown assassins whose bullets brought about an abrupt end to her investigation into the weapons being smuggled into South Africa.

He shivers. That was then, though. 1988. The dark, dying days of apartheid. Government spies behaving badly (or so goes the official narrative). But at least one tenacious investigative journalist had concluded it was more complicated, wasn't quite so black and white – that the dirt she'd been digging up wasn't just a stain on the apartheid government, but something that certain of her comrades – colleagues in the Congress – preferred be kept secret too.

He pictures The Knife in Paris, 24 years younger than he is now, a silenced pistol wedged into one coat pocket. Was it him? Unlikely, perhaps, but not entirely implausible, no. His tread would've been lighter then. Clip, clip his shoes went. Step by step, getting nearer to Dulcie, Dulcie who might have recognized him if it hadn't been for his baclava, Dulcie who was humming at the top of the stairs as she flicked through the post, a ring of keys twirling on her index finger.

Adam walks quickly, glancing around. No one cares – no one is interested in him. What would an assassin look like? Probably like he didn't care, like he hadn't noticed him. And then –

BANG!

He ducks. He is still alive. He is crouched down, looking over his shoulder. He stands up, laughs. It is just an old Datsun sputtering along; the sound must've been its exhaust.

Is this what it will be like now? Wondering, waiting? Is Zandile right? Are the threats just idle – bullies trying to force them to back down?

He is at the police station for almost three hours, most of it waiting in a queue. When he is finally in front of the policewoman on duty, she writes down his statement in careful capital letters. She places the three notes in a clear plastic bag, tells him the detective will call him when he is next available. Adam asks her about the shit.

'Just wash it off,' she tells him. He can't tell if she is amused or disdainful. Maybe she just doesn't care.

His phone begins ringing as he walks back to the office.

'Good day, is that Adam Miller?'

'Yes.'

He stops at the zebra crossing, waits for the lights to change.

'Adam, Ronald Simpson here, I'm an old friend of Lindiwe Sithole. She gave me your number. I'm a media lawyer.'

'Hi.'

The little man is still red, and so he decides to run – the cars are still far away enough.

'I see that Minister Lindela is threatening legal action if you don't drop the story.'

'Yes.'

'Well, I just wanted to let you know, if it does come to that, I am happy to represent you. Pro bono.'

Adam has slowed down; he sees a bench, leans against it.

'Are you there?'

'Sorry.' A sob escapes, juddering through him. 'Sorry. Yes, thank you.'

'Are you OK?'

'I'm... fine.'

'It's OK to be taking strain. It's perfectly natural to.' The voice is smoother than soap. Deliciously serene.

'Just remember this isn't just your battle. I'm sure Lindiwe's told you that. The behaviour of the ruling party is outrageous. We need to make sure that it doesn't think it can just trample on this country's freedoms.'

'Yes,' Adam gasps. 'It's just – well, I wish it wasn't me. I wish it wasn't my business partner, Lindi's daughter. I'm so scared she'll get hurt.'

'It'll be fine, Adam,' the man says firmly.

'That's what she says. But how do you both know?'

'It's just posturing. We've seen it before. Well, not quite as extreme as this in the new democratic dispensation, admittedly. But, I'm afraid it's par for the course. Just hang in there. And if I can offer you some reassurance, I don't think you'll be taken to court. All this is bluster. They know they don't stand a chance of winning the case.'

Max has returned, calmer. Joan is out, and that worries him: where can she be, what is she doing, who is she talking to? His head aches; thoughts have been swirling down, blanketing him in blessed incomprehension. He steps numbly towards the kitchen, puts the kettle on. He will not leave just yet. He will make tea. While the kettle boils he goes upstairs.

The iPad is on the coffee table. Was that where he left it? Or did he leave it on the couch? Has Joan been looking at it? He laughs – there is a lock-code; she can't have looked at his browsing history, even if she had tried to.

He searches on Google News, spots the headline Black wounds, white oblivion. The link takes him to *New Era*'s website. He starts reading.

To foreign eyes, and white ones locally, the debate engulfing the publication of "The President" might seem entirely disproportionate. It is, after all, just a short story in an obscure online literary journal imagining the president of a country (perhaps not even our own) having sex with a rent boy. But to see it this way only reveals the blinkered ignorance that so many white people still have of the traumatic wounds that persist after centuries of racial oppression. Is the story intentionally racist? We may never know. But what perhaps matters more than that is the inescapable fact that it could have – and indeed has – been perceived as such.

Black people see this as an attack – on their masculinity and on their dignity. This is because culturally, many still equate homosexuality with something that is weak, feminine and "unAfrican" – incompatible, in other words, with their culture and traditions. They also see it as an "import", being imposed on them by European neo-colonialism. It is easy to brush away such views as ridiculous if you've never been oppressed. It is easy to claim that there is nothing wrong with being gay or feminine or that homosexuality has been present on this continent for centuries. But this misses the point. The point is that centuries of subjugation and oppression in this country was designed to quash and demean African masculine identity. A story – written presumably by a white writer and published by a white editor – imagining a gay Black president serves as a powerful and painful reminder of this emasculation.

And the story goes even further: the Black president character is sodomised by a white rent boy. The metaphor is obvious: whites are still subjugating Blacks, even those in positions of power. As the rhetoric we have seen this week shows, many Black political figures believe the Struggle against racist oppression is not over – that although whites might no longer wield immense political power, they still have the power to hurt and they do this wantonly. *Vula* and its publishers suggest that the story aims to foster tolerance of sexual minorities (which is indeed a noble aim). As outrage has grown, they have doubled-down with a crusade to protect the freedom of expression they argue is now being imperilled by people's justifiable anger. But whether well-intentioned or not, their white oblivion is only making a complicated and difficult situation worse. The publication of the story means that gays and other people who self-identify under the LGBT umbrella will only be further marginalised, pushed further away from acceptance. They will be perceived by the majority as disrespectful to this country's president, its elders and its traditions. And the insulting reminder of the humiliations wrought by centuries of white oppression does much to undermine reconciliation between races.

Freedom of expression needs to be wielded carefully, with sensitivity. Instead of being oblivious, whites must be mindful of the lingering hurt which remains, and the importance of the need to enhance the dignity of all – in particular, those who were once oppressed.

If we are to grow as a nation, artistic expression should not trump nation-building and social cohesion. *Vula* should remove the story and apologise – not merely to the Blacks of this country who have been so hurt, but to everyone committed to building a bright future for all.

GEORGINA PHILLIPS IS A PROFESSOR OF GENDER STUDIES AT THE UNIVERSITY OF CAPE TOWN, AND HEADS UP THE UNIVERSITY'S NEWLY ESTABLISHED GENDER POLICY & GOVERNANCE UNIT.

Georgina Phillips! Max shakes his head. He would love to shout – how dare you speak for an entire race (one that isn't even yours!)? Fuck your false pity and your smug assumptions. You never felt the hurt; it wasn't yours to feel, so don't speak as if you know it intimately. And don't let the pain, the pain you've never felt firsthand, justify your call to quash my voice, my story, *me*. Just because you want more government funding for your policy unit, just because you want to be in my dad's good – best – books (and possibly his bed). What a bootlicking, brownnosing bitch. It fucking stinks!

There is a pause while Minister Lindela's secretary connects him. Then, the now-familiar baritone is booming, 'Adam! How are you doing?'

'Not very well, Minister.'

'I'm sorry to hear that.'

'Minister, when I arrived at work this morning, shit had been smeared across the windows. Three threatening letters were in the mail. More arrived at lunchtime. I've had some strange calls.'

'That is unfortunate, Adam.'

'To say the least, Minister. I'd like to know whether you or your government has anything to do with this?'

'I'm shocked you felt the need to ask! Unlike our authoritarian apartheid predecessors, this democratically elected government has the highest respect for due process; we're certainly not involved in anything untoward. Of course it's extremely unfortunate that this is happening. But I don't think you should be surprised. Your publication has demeaned a beloved leader held in high regard by many millions. Did you really think people would just take this kind of disrespect lying down? Did you think there'd be no consequences? People are angry. Extremely angry. And one can hardly blame them.'

'We could be killed. Do you realise that, Minister? Our lives are at risk. If something happens to Zandile or myself – you've got blood on your hands. Goodbye.'

'Adam,' Zandile says when he's hung up. 'Calm down a bit, OK? I know this is godawful, but outrage is not going to help.'

'It's ridiculous, Zandile. It makes me so fucking angry.'

'Why don't you take the day off? Watch a movie or go for a run or something. You need to decompress.'

He shakes his head. He resents her equanimity – why isn't she angry? Why isn't she scared?

'I assume you've heard about the Youth League press conference which just happened.'

He nods. 'I don't get why you're so calm, Zandile. On Friday, they're going to march on us.'

She shrugs. 'Let them march. So what. Let them get it off their chest. By the weekend, everything will be forgotten.'

He wants to ask her – How do you know that? How can you be so sure? But he doesn't. He goes to the kitchen, finds a mop and a bucket, which he starts filling with water. He adds a squirt of dish soap.

'Where you going?' calls Zandile as he's about to head downstairs with the bucket.

'I'm going to clean the windows out front.'

'Letitia can do it. She's coming in tomorrow, remember?'

'This is our shit – we need to deal with it,' he sighs. There's no way can he ask the lady who comes into clean their office once a week to remove faeces – human faeces – from a window.

In the end he does decide to leave work early. If he stays, he risks snapping again at Zandile (or conducting another intemperate phone conversation). He has emailed their winery client informing them that the three tasting notes he was supposed to revise today he will get to early tomorrow.

At the flat he tries to read a novel. He can't concentrate; he keeps reading the same paragraph again and again. He checks his phone. Nothing: no calls, no messages. Is this the eye of the storm – or the calm before it?

When he gets back to the flat from a run, he sees there are three missed calls from Charl, the winery's marketing director, and a voicemail asking him to phone him. Were those tasting notes that urgent? Or is this about something else? He queasily dials Charl.

'Adam. *Jissie*, man. Your side project... this *Vula* thing. Take that story down, immediately. *Asseblief*.'

'What? *Vula* has nothing to do with the winery. God knows I've tried hard enough to get you guys to sponsor it.'

'Thank goodness we never did. You've got to remove this porno president story ASAP.'

Adam decides to play dumb. 'Why?'

'Come on, man. You really can't see what's at stake? Every South African embassy on the planet serves our wines at the dinners they host – wines with descriptions you've written, with labels designed by Zandile. It's only a matter of time before someone points out that Lekgotla the branding agency is the publisher of *Vula*. That Lekgotla's biggest client is us. And our biggest client is the South African government. The longer the story stays up, the more likely it is that the dots get joined. It's not terribly hard. It's right there – for anyone who's looking closely enough to see. You link from *Vula* to Lekgotla's website, where you proudly include the work you've done for the winery under featured work. I bet our competitors are probably on the phone to the minister right now; they're probably sending him screenshots of this as we speak. The national airline could drop us too. The chair of its board is very close to the president. If she catches wind... that's thousands of litres of wine down the drain.'

'Fine,' he replies.

'You'll take it down?'

'No. Of course not.' He should've had some orange juice before calling – his post-run, pre-dinner brain is all mushy, thoughts melting into each other. What is he saying? Did he really just tell Charl to fuck off? He didn't actually use the word 'fuck' did he?

'Adam, do you not understand what I'm saying? If you don't remove it, we can't carry on working with you.'

He waited. He closed his eyes. 'I have an idea. I can remove the references to the winery on Lekgotla's website. You won't be listed as one of our clients.'

'That's not good enough, Adam. All we need is some hack from *New Era* using the Wayback Machine to dredge up proof that we're a client of yours. The only solution is for the story to go. If you want us to remain a client, that's what it's going to take, *finish and klaar.*'

Adam sits down, shivering. 'Can I chat to Zandile, please?' He'll take a hot shower, put on warm clothes, and call her.

'Delete it, Adam! I'm giving you until 9 tomorrow morning.'

Later, he's forgotten, almost forgotten. He and Jaco have moved on to whisky. The two bottles of wine they've already emptied sit on their table at the Power and the Glory. He feels his phone buzzing in his shirt pocket, fishes it out (it almost drops). Zandile's name is flashing on the screen. Adam knocks his way between the tables, answers it outside.

'Why weren't you answering your phone? The winery wants to ditch us,' he says. 'They say we have to remove the story or they won't work with us.'

'That's pathetic.'

'We have to take the story down, Zandile. It's just not worth it anymore. We can't afford to lose such a big client.'

'Ad, have you been drinking?'

'Just a little bit. Seriously, though. We really need to take it down.'

'Let's chat about it tomorrow morning.'

'But they need an answer tomorrow. By nine.'

'They can wait.'

'Honestly. You think this is a fucking joke. You're not taking this seriously! Do you want us to end up broke?'

'Ad... Let's chat in the morning. Look after yourself tonight, OK?'

He hangs up without saying goodbye.

WEDNESDAY

[23]

Max has had a troubled night – waking, waiting, then tripping back to sleep. He's awake again as dawn inches in over the rooftops' dark geometry; he stretches, then goes downstairs. Joan has a moka pot like Adam's. He fetches the ground coffee from the fridge, pours water into its metal base. When the coffee has been heaped into the canister and the top screwed on, he puts it on the hob.

The aroma, when it comes, sends him right back to that morning; it is so far away, but it is right here, when he stands next to Adam as the batter firms up on the pan, and Sarah Vaughn's voice surrounds them.

He feels a bursting. Adam is tough. He will be OK. Hopefully.

He sits down with his iPad, mug at his side. Another Google search. So much outrage. Where is the sanity? There are some reasonable voices, it is true. A constitutional law expert is calling on Minister Lindela to resign. In his blog, he describes him as 'the greatest threat to our constitutional democracy' and 'playing fast and loose with the safety of those who are different or dare to brook dissent'. And then, there is a retired former cabinet minister, Monty Tshabalala, who has written an op-ed for the *Daily Times*.

The publication of a controversial story depicting a state president as homosexual offers a litmus test for our young democracy – and we are not faring well. The ruling party's rhetoric – and that of its petulant Youth League – emphasise words like "freedom", "dignity" and "democracy". It is interesting how these words have been cynically misappropriated in a bid to stifle dissent and quash creative expression.

There is nothing wrong with a president being homosexual. The fact that a story depicting this is interpreted as "offensive" and "demeaning" exposes the entrenched prejudice our rulers have towards sexual minorities. It is thoroughly in keeping with the desire that Minister Lindela has recently expressed to curtail the rights of gay people to love those they wish to.

I know something about oppression. I was jailed for several years

in the very same prison that our dear president was incarcerated. Why was I fighting? Because I hoped that one day I would live in a society where we could all live – and love – freely. I fought for the freedom of all. Black and white. Straight and gay. Men and women.

Invited by our first democratically elected president to join his cabinet in 1994, I served with pride in his administration, committed to building a truly liberated society, one where we could boldly express our authentic selves without the risk of harm or censure. With the promulgation of our new constitution in 1996, our nation was at the vanguard of human rights – globally. This remarkable document, this moral lodestar, was the first constitution in the world to ban discrimination on the basis of sexual orientation.

It is 16 years later, and how times have changed! Human rights are no longer in vogue. Persecution and prejudice are making a sinister comeback. And all because principles have been forsaken in the pursuit of ever more power. Yes, indeed. I believe Minister Lindela, and – I'm sure – the president who appointed him, are anxious to turn the ruling party's popular mandate into perpetual, untrammelled power. Victory at the ballot box is not enough. Control – of debate, ideas, people – is the desired aim. It has taken me several years to realise this. And even longer to speak out. I feel a wrenching. The liberation movement I have devotedly served – first as a foot soldier, then later as an MP and as a cabinet minister – has always been a broad church. But, instead of pursuing and advancing liberty, it has become a monstrous machine where power (and the patronage that begets yet more power) is the goal.

I have observed the statements made by the Rottweiler who leads the Youth League. This toddler knows nothing of the fight for freedom or the sacrifices that were made for it; he was in nappies when the old dispensation finally collapsed under the weight of our mighty movement's Long Walk to Freedom.

His handlers should know better than to unleash him, gnashing and foaming, onto the body politic. But we all know that power corrupts, and we should – I suppose – not be surprised. Nevertheless, is it unfair of me to have wished for something better, to believe that even our very own president would return from exile and embrace the dream of freedom for all, instead of the nightmare of oppression by a

Max remembers Monty – the last time he saw him was at Walter Sisulu's funeral in 2003; he and his wife had sat next to Max and his dad. He'd noticed Max coughing during the singing of the national anthem, had offered him two boiled sweets which he had gratefully accepted.

And now Monty has written this. He could almost weep. He empties and washes the moka pot and his mug. It doesn't take him long to pack.

He finds a postcard in his rucksack. Pulls a fineliner out of his jeans' pocket and scribbles a brief goodbye note which he leaves leaning against the kettle so she'll see it when she makes her tea. The front door clicks shut behind him. The sun already seems high. Contrails crosshatch the sky. The street is alive: cars disgorge children outside the school; a rubbish truck scuttles forward. The collectors shout; one passes him at the gate, winks.

A man with an afro walks on the opposite pavement, earphones in his ears, eyes on the ground in front of him. Is his absorption too deliberate?

Max waits for him to disappear from view. He is standing on the pavement now. He breathes deeply. Who here could it be? Or is he free? There is nothing he can do but walk. He turns left, heading away from Shepherds Bush Road. The street quietens. A lady is walking her poodle, which zigzags across the pavement, nose to the flagstones.

Max tugs the straps of his rucksack, lets it settle onto his back. He walks faster; the road curves, past an old brick warehouse. Then there are more railings, the wide bay windows and smart doors of terraced houses. He glances behind him. If someone is following, he cannot see him.

Adam knows that Zandile knows he's sorry, but he mumbles an apology anyway when she hugs him. She looks up at him, brow crinkling with concern, then lets go, silently. They take their mugs to the couch. She's found a plate for the two almond croissants she bought on the way to the office, and at first they just sit there, tugging tufts of pastry loose and putting them in their mouths.

'What are we going to do?' he eventually says.

'We can't fold,' she replies.

'That's almost two-thirds of our income we're kissing goodbye, Zandile. We can't afford to do *Vula* without that money. And – we'll have barely enough to live off if we do.'

She sips her tea, puts the mug down. 'I know it's a worry, but we'll find other clients. We'll keep going. We'll find a way. All I know is that we can't capitulate – the whole country's watching. If we surrender then what are they going to try do next?'

'And what if no other clients want to work with us? What if they're all as scared as the winery?'

'Then we try get funding for *Vula* – and do that full-time.'

'Who's going to fund us?'

She shrugs. 'The Goethe-Insitut? Pro Helvetia? The Scandis? I don't know. I'm sure we'll find the money.'

She's living in a dream. He wants to shake her awake. 'And when it comes out we're funded by Europeans, how is that going to look? They're already claiming we're imperialist stooges. If we get foreign funding they will say that proves their point.'

She takes his hand. 'OK. I'm asking you to trust me. Let's just take this a day at a time. This is all going to blow over soon, and people – new people – will want to work with us again; people who actually support what we do, that have the same values we have. It'll be fine. But we absolutely can't fold. We have to hold onto "The President" – the precedent created if we don't is just too ghastly.'

He squeezes her hand, gets up. 'Fine. You tell Charl that we're not going to take it down.'

'OK. It will be my pleasure. Frankly I can't bear the thought of continuing to work with someone that spineless anyway. You write a statement for the blog. Tell the world we're standing firm. You don't have to mention the winery. But I think it's important people know that we're not going to waver.'

He takes the mugs to the kitchen, adds them to the bunch of dirty ones in the sink.

'Isn't Letitia coming today?'

When he comes back into the office, Zandile is glowering at her phone.

'Fuck,' she says, looking up.

'What?'

'She sent a message while we were chatting. Someone threw a stone through her window last night. She says it's better if she stays at home today. She says people know who she works for.'

He shakes his head. 'How the fuck do people know? I just don't get it.' He sits down heavily on his seat. 'What if something happens to her now? That's going to be our fault, Zandile. Fuck!'

Zandile is still staring at her phone. 'I'm sure nothing will happen.' She sounds less certain than previously.

If going to London was wise, staying with Joan was stupid. Max should have known The Knife was two steps ahead, always. He had allowed himself to feel safe – stupid. He can't be certain that The Knife contacted her, that he's asked her to monitor him – but it makes too much sense. Disappearing from home – it was only a matter of time before The Knife became suspicious.

He climbs off the Tube at St Paul's again. He is not in a hurry so he heads into a coffee shop. There is a new post on *Vula*'s blog.

LONG LIVE 'THE PRESIDENT'

The past 48 hours have witnessed an extraordinary intensification of hatred directed at this publication and at Gabriel Roberts, the author of "The President", the short story we published last week Thursday. We have seen a deluge of death threats pouring in. The first one I read shocked me deeply – I couldn't quite believe it when I saw it. Now there are at least twenty in the letterbox.

Of course, I'm not the only one on the receiving end. I can't bear to repeat the screaming rage that my business partner and best friend, Zandile, has been receiving; even someone as ardently in favour of freedom of speech as myself flinches when reading the text messages and the emails she has been sent. I am accused of being a racist. She is being accused of being a traitor. The latter is, in the eyes of many, a far worse crime. Yesterday, excrement was smeared across the ground-level windows (incidentally belonging to other tenants – sorry about that, neighbours). Our domestic helper had a stone lobbed through her window last night. People are very, very angry. And, to be honest, we are very, very afraid.

Minister Lindela is determined to force us to take down the story. He insists that its presence on *Vula* is the antithesis of freedom and democracy. As you will know, he has given us until 12pm tomorrow to remove it. He has told me personally that he is playing by the rules. But is he? I find it incredibly difficult to accept that someone who ostensibly places such a great emphasis on dignity, freedom and democracy remains completely shtum about the threats we are re-ceiving. He is deeply concerned about the dignity of our president, and yet has no qualms about watching the dignity of myself and oth-ers be undermined through threats of torture, assault and murder. Clearly some animals are more equal than others.

Now the ruling party's Youth League will be marching to us. It has launched a witch-hunt to find out who and where "Gabriel Roberts" really is.

Yes, Minister Lindela claims to be playing by the rules. But his persecution is by proxy. Through being silent, he implicitly condones the behaviour of the cyber trolls and of the Congress Youth League. What will they do when they march on this building? They will not find Gabriel Roberts. But if they were to – what then? They say they will teach him about democracy, about freedom. What does this entail? As a disillusioned Monty Tshabalala explained in the *Daily Times* this morning, the ruling party and its thuggish accessories have stripped these words – "democracy", "freedom" – of meaning. If this is their version of democracy then we are fucked. Might is not automatically right. This morning, I suggested to Zandile that we take down the story so that the threats might abate, so that life might get back to normal. But – to her credit – she's a lot feistier than I am. Zandile believes it would be a victory for intolerance to remove the story. She is 100% right.

So, to everyone who demands that we remove the story, to everyone who says we deserve to die: we will not be backing down. We will not surrender to intolerance. This country has had a violent, tragic history of persecution and oppression. Zandile and myself were both young enough to be spared the experience of this. Our generation was nicknamed "Mandela's Children". We have both grown up in what we believed to be a free country – a country that so many in the very ruling party which now attempts to censor and persecute us fought to liberate. This is not just about our lives, or our right to express ourselves. The intolerance directed at us places that very liberation under threat because it is being waged by those in power. It sets a dreadful precedent. If *Vula* can't publish what it wants, if Gabriel Roberts can't write what he likes – if we are told by the ruling party and its useful idiots what we can and cannot say, then our liberation is dead. Oppression will have triumphed once more, and the ruling party will continue to dictate to us, the people of this country, what we can think, feel and say. And so we will carry on the fight – for freedom, for tolerance. "The President" will live on.

ADAM MILLER, EDITOR

In the end Max chooses Paddington. It has a comforting number of lines leading away from its three white circles – after the call, he can disappear; the city is his oyster. Only one of the payphones is operational so he has to wait while a woman shrouded in black wails into the receiver. The sun is gone; he shivers. Looks around. Too many people. Anyone: it could be anyone or no one and in this he takes some comfort – the possibilities have submerged him; he is floating in their flood.

When the woman has finally finished her call, Max goes up to the payphone, inserts several pound coins, and dials. Nomsa, his dad's assistant, picks up on the third ring.

'It's Max. I need to speak to my father. Is he around?'

'Max! It's been ages, dearie. The minister is out at the moment. He had a meeting in Parliament earlier, but he's due back in the office in the next

20 minutes or so. I would try him on his cell.'

Max thanks her, hangs up. He needs to go. Nomsa has been briefed, probably. She's been told – keep him there. Tell him to call the minister's mobile. Easier to track that way. The longer he's faffing, the faster they find him. Or. Is he – he might be just being ridiculous. It's a possibility. But why risk it?

Trafalgar Square has far fewer pigeons than he remembers – when Joan was holding his one hand, and he was scattering seed with the other so that splotches of grey coalesced around them; he could feel the wind of their wings in his face as he giggled and Joan shrieked.

Where have they gone? Perhaps into the eaves, hiding and dry, sensible things knowing they won't be fed today (everyone appears to be en route elsewhere). He stands near the fountain, the lone dawdler wishing he had his jacket on. Walks closer to the High Commission – South Africa's High Commission.

Closer. Closer. Only the road separates him and the building now. A bus reddens the view, no pillars or statues for a few seconds. And then again – the diplomatic outpost's grey grandeur, its waiting steps. It is almost tempting to walk over, to climb up them. He can see the journey now – onto marbled floors, the whispers to a man wearing a headpiece. The southward call while he waits. Waiting for a command, a hushed discussion, and then – what would happen then?

He doesn't know. It is pure, silly conjecture. It is not in the plot – he would never write it so. He turns, crosses the square. A gust carries the fountain's spray, it mixes with the drizzle; he speeds up. There is a payphone next to a bus stop. He pushes the cold metal buttons that make up his father's mobile number and the dialling tone begins.

'What the hell are you doing in England?'

Max tells his dad he felt like going on holiday. That he's been missing Joan; it had been years since they've seen each other, after all.

'What about university? And why didn't you tell me? I was getting worried.'

Max apologises.

'When will you be coming back?'

Max hesitated. 'Soon.'

'What do you mean 'soon'? What's the date of your return flight?'

'Next week Monday,' he lied.
'Call me when you're back. You're coming for dinner.'

THURSDAY

[24]

They have pushed the world away, hidden it beyond the door. Both their phones are off. Last night they made a lamb casserole, then watched *Roman Holiday*; Adam fell asleep snuggled up next to Zandile as the credits rolled; when he woke up, he was alone, with a blanket laid over him and flames still spitting in the grate.

Today, after fried eggs on toast, they've watched *Under the Tuscan Sun*. Then, while Zandile made hot chocolate, Adam let Bokassa out, watching the cat tread disdainfully into the drizzle. They are about half way through *Notting Hill* when the landline rings.

'Fuck, do you think the press have found your number?' Adam says, when film has been paused.

Zandile goes to the kitchen. The ringing stops.

'Yes...,' she says. 'Sorry... I'm sorry, Mom... I know... Shit, are you sure? I'll check this end too... I don't believe it... Yes, Mom, I will... OK, love you, bye.'

Zandile comes in to the living room, hands on hips. 'That was my mom. We've been hacked.'

'What?'

'Mom says that when you go onto the website, all it says now is

THE PRESIDENT IS <u>NOT</u> GAY. EVIL GAYS <u>REPENT</u>.'

Adam's legs piston easily as he heads towards his flat. It is good to be out, in the blustery sun. He is smiling; it is a smile he hadn't dared show Zandile earlier. Now she has become the outraged one, he the calm consoler. He had not admitted to her he was glad – glad the site had been destroyed, glad that when he phoned their internet service provider, the customer service director (who he was eventually put through to) point blank refused to fix the site.

Yes, he is glad "The President" has gone; things can go back to the way they were, now; perhaps the winery will work with them again. Tomorrow's march will surely be cancelled.

The letters will stop (he wonders how many more have accumulated since they left the office yesterday). The calls from journalists for comment will dry up. The madness will end. He relishes the prospect. He has done his bit – both he and Zandile have done their bit, made a stand.

And now it is over, thank God. They have not surrendered; they have just been beaten.

'We should publish the story somewhere else – like on our Tumblr,' Zandile had suggested as he was about to leave the office.

'Nah, let's leave it be. We've made our point.'

She had not demurred, thankfully.

Now she is on her way to fetch Bjorn from the airport; Adam will write a statement for *Vula*'s blog when he gets home. They've decided their phones will remain off. There will be no more quotes given to journalists; no more radio interviews. They will post what they want to say on Tumblr – that is all.

He unlocks the flat door. A window in the lounge is open, slightly. He goes up to it, brows knitted. He never leaves windows open when he goes out. He looks around. Everything is normal. He sniffs. Nothing. Nothing is different.

He goes to the bedroom. The narrow table next to his bed, where he normally leaves his laptop, is clear – there is just the mug from yesterday morning. Did he put it away? No, of course he hasn't – he never puts his laptop anywhere else.

'Fuck,' he mutters.

He puts the wooden chair down in front of the cupboard, stands on it, pulls the top doors open. There are his towels, neatly rolled. And his medicine chest. He sighs – the wooden box, the one where he keeps his hard drive with all his computer back-ups is there. He takes it out, unclips the lid, opens it.

The hard drive has gone.

Zandile refuses to fucking believe him, insists Adam must have left his laptop at the office.

'Check tomorrow – it'll be there,' she says when he calls her.

'What about the hard drive? I've been burgled, I'm sure of it.'

'Relax, friend. You probably put it in a different place the last time you backed up.'

He'd wanted to leave her and Bjorn to have a night alone together; Bjorn has been in Stockholm for a whole week. But he is scared, and she must sense this, because she insists he comes over for dinner and a sleepover as soon as he's finished the blog post.

In another coffee shop, Max checks Twitter again. @readVula has only one new tweet: Site is down. *Vula* has been hacked. Appended is a link to a post on Vula's blog:

'The President' is dead.

This morning, a cyber attack destroyed *Vula*'s website. Our internet service provider assured us that, under normal circumstances, it would have been able to restore the site's functionality within 24 hours. But: these are not normal circumstances. Its customer service email address and call centre have been bombarded with threats. The ISP has decided that, to avoid risking the safety of its staff, it will not be able to continue to provide us with hosting services. And so, "The President" is dead. We have considered publishing the short story on a website hosted outside of the country – this can, after all, be done within a matter of minutes. But after deliberating this afternoon, we have decided to leave it. The piece has served its purpose – it has got the nation conversing, even if it feels like

Max checks the headlines on Google News; there is a long list of results about the hacking. But the newest is an article from NewsLine: "We will still march" – Youth League.

'Even though the story is no longer viewable, we must show this gay white rubbish that they must not insult our president and our democracy,' the Youth League chair is quoted saying. 'We are bringing the democratic revolution to Gabriel Roberts!'

As they wait for pizza to reheat in the oven, Adam tells Zandile he doesn't think it is a good idea for them to come to the office tomorrow.

Zandile demurs. 'We can't cower. We have to stand up to this. Nothing will happen, trust me. They will march; they will wave their banners; they will get their free lunch. And then they'll go home. Life will carry on.'

'We still have to be careful.'

'Well then, why don't *you* go into hiding?'

Adam rolls his eyes.

She stretches her hand forward, gripping his. 'I think it's wonderful that you want to keep me safe. But I'm not going to let this crap disrupt my life.'

He nods, silently.

"I have to prove to myself that I can live my life here freely. Otherwise, if I am so intimidated, then I might as well fuck off to Sweden, don't you think?"

FRIDAY

[25]

The first joggers come past, their footfalls trampling lightly on Max's sleep. His lids ignore the brightening sky for a while longer. And then he sits up on the bench, rubbing his eyes, letting them drift beyond the railings to the glimmering river.

Today is the day.

Under the dripping avenue of oaks, uniformed children slump their way towards school; squirrels dart away from striding office workers. It all feels so normal – this could be the start of any other day. Adam passes Parliament and St George's Cathedral. The sun has broken free; there are gaps of blue now, hoping between clouds.

There is no shit on the downstairs windows, he notes, as he unlocks the office's front door. He doesn't check the letterbox. He runs up the stairs. The office is normal – the computers, the whiteboard with Post-its, the books and magazines: everything is as it should be.

Zandile enters, unwinding the scarf from around her neck. He must be looking worried because she goes up to him, hugs him, says, 'It's going to be OK.'

Adam remains tensed up. 'What if something happens?'

'What do you think will happen? It's simple, Ad. They'll say some speeches. And then they'll go home. Sooner or later they'll have to.'

He nods.

'Trust me, it's going to be OK.'

Adam's laptop is not in the office. He has searched the shelves for his hard drive, too; it is nowhere to be found. He switches on his iMac without saying anything to Zandile. He has given up. She will tell him they're both probably at his flat after all; he should double-check to make sure before anything is said publicly about the theft.

He sighs. He knows that fear is only useful up to a certain point. Beyond it, it has no purpose; all it promises is paralysis and pain. He can be cautious, careful, but ultimately life will be inscribed the way it is written. He just has to face it. He looks at Zandile – she's scribbling in her notebook, looking at her computer screen, brainstorming possible future clients – clients to fill the winery-sized hole their income statement will soon have. She's thinking about the future. There will be a future – this too shall pass. The marchers will come, they will go, life will carry on.

It will all be OK.

It's probably over by now but Max doesn't know, has not looked. It was enough to know the march was happening. It was enough to know he could do nothing to stop it. Yet still, he feels responsible. Like he was the one leading the charge – was there a charge? There might have been. He can see it, the marchers coursing up to Lekgotla's office.

He has crossed the bridge. He has walked down to the building, the dark glass-covered one. He is inside. He can hear footfalls on polished stone, hushed voices. He looks up at the rows of balconies. A security guard stands at a turnstile.

'I'm here to see Juliette Findlay.'

He is allowed to enter. The man escorts him to the front desk.

'He's here to see Ms Findlay,' the guard tells the receptionist.

'Your name?'

'Max Smythe. I'm a journalist with *New Era*.'

The security guard walks back to his post as the lady's nail extensions tap-tap against a telephone console. She speaks into an earpiece: 'Smythe. Max. Here. Says he's a journalist?' She nods. 'Won't you take a seat, sir?'

Max settles into an armchair, takes out his iPad. Now is the time. He publishes the draft post on therealgabrielroberts.tumblr.com. He emails the link to Adam. On Twitter, his handle, @TheRealGabrielRoberts, is ready. He types I am the son of @MinisterRuralAffairs Richard Lindela – I am the REAL Gabriel Roberts. This is what I have to say: and the link.

'Hello, Max.'

He looks up to see a blonde woman peering at him through angular spectacles.

'Lovely to meet you.'

'Likewise.'

'Let's head on up, shall we?'

The lift doors close. He feels a surge; is it just the lift, or is it something else? He doesn't have to worry anymore. There is a sense of lightness; he is floating; it makes him smile.

'Well, thank you so much for coming to visit us. We're so excited about CanResource's expansion into your country, and I can't wait to tell you all about our plans, particularly from a social responsibility point of view. As you know, we really put that at the heart of the way we do business.'

Max nods. The doors open. They are on the top floor. Across from an empty stretch of carpet is a café with couches and little tables surrounded by uncomfortable looking stools.

'Do you mind if I go to the toilet?'

'Not at all. Let me sort out a coffee for you in the meantime. What can I get you? Flat white?'

'That's perfect. No sugar, please.'

In the gents, he goes to a stall, starts unzipping his jeans, laughs: why bother pissing? Talk about pointless. He zips back up then takes out his iPad. He wants to check – is Adam OK? But there is no time. He lifts the cistern's lid with one hand, drops the iPad into the water with the other.

Enough dawdling, no need to wash hands, now is the time, let's get it over with. *Finish and klaar.* He wipes his palms, damp and cool, on his jeans. Sees Juliette carrying a tray with two coffees. Turns to look straight ahead. He counts the steps to the railing. His eighth gently touches the low wall beneath it. His hands hold tightly as he stares dazedly downwards. It is clear – the marble at the bottom is blank, clean, empty, a story waiting to be written.

He lifts one foot to the top of the wall, feeling the muscles stretching as it rises. He turns quickly, sees Juliette's mouth falling slowly. She is putting the tray down, almost dropping it. Her mouth is opening. Maybe words come out – he isn't sure, because all he can hear now is the blood bumping against his eardrums as he lifts his other foot.

It wasn't OK.

That is why they are sitting here, in a creamy-walled boardroom, sipping sugary tea.

That is why a consular official is carefully dabbing a Dettol-soaked cotton bud against Zandi's cheek. That is why 15 minutes ago they were running like rats along the pavement. Would they have been spotted if they had calmly walked out from the courtyard into the street? It is impossible to say. All they know is that some of the marchers – those too lazy to cross the threshold, lolling with banners and placards at the conquered entrance instead – spotted Adam and Zandile turn out from the courtyard. The more observant among them saw the

pair join the flow of pedestrians. There was shouting. Adam turned, saw placards drifting to the ground, hands clenching into fists, legs springing forward.

'Run!'

Zandile was barefoot – Adam couldn't tell if she had lost or abandoned
her ballet pumps; he just wished she was faster. They leapt over the boxes of
fruit for sale, weaved between people. It was a dance – around a woman on
her cellphone, around two men staring upwards. Another man wagged his
finger at them as they approached.

Adam turned his head again – marchers holding pangas. The gap between them was shrinking. He pulled Zandile off the kerb; they ignored the
hooting cars, ignored the miracle of not getting hit.

'Come.' He yanked her warm, sticky hand into a side street. There were
fewer people here.

Adam could hear a scream – had a car hit one of the marchers crossing
the road?

The Swedish consulate was in front of them. The double doors hissed open.

'Help! Help! We're being chased!' It was Zandile. The doors shut behind
them. 'Please, lock the doors!'

The security guard remained still, impassive.

'Please!'

He pressed a button. Faces were appearing at the glass. Adam stared at
them; there were five or six. One lifted a panga, pretending to strike.

Adam closed his eyes. When he opened them, a woman with pursed lips
was sauntering towards them.

'Can you please come upstairs?'

'We're – ' The words don't come out. He is hoarse. He coughs.

'We know who you are. We've been watching the march on TV. Please.
Come this way.'

After the blood has been wiped away and the tea has been finished, Zandile
starts to cry. She does so quietly: she does not want words now – just Adam's
hand, which she holds tightly.

She has been told her mom is on the way, with the lawyer, Ronald Simpson.
They will come through the back entrance, where the diplomats park, just
in case there is trouble out front. The windows span the height of the room,
almost. Adam has been standing, watching the street. He saw the police van
arrive, saw the policeman's hand jutting through the window, gesticulating.

There were no arrests; the seven men just walked away, loping back towards the square. The police departed soon after, and Adam returned to his seat at the conference table.

'Sorry?'

There is a man, predictably blonde and Viking-tall, who had come into the room a few minutes earlier. He is sitting next to Adam, elbows resting on the birch table, one set of his fingertips touching the other.

'I was saying we need to figure out the next steps.' He turns to Zandile. 'But perhaps let's wait until your husband gets here first.'

The next steps? Adam's world has broken; there is a gulf. Maybe the cracks were there, when the shit was smeared on the window, when the death threats came, when the site was hacked. But now it is different; it can never be the same. His mind is fizzing. The next steps. What is happening now at the square? What does the office look like? The place must be trashed. He can see cracked computer screens, and ripped-up books. Or maybe the protesters have looted them, shoving them into the tote bags hanging on the doorknob. Take Orwell, fuckers – *Animal Farm*, *1984*. Burn them if you must, but fucking read them first.

He cannot go back.

'Adam.' He looks up. The deputy consul-general has put away the first aid kit; she is hovering next to him with an iPad. 'You don't have your phone on you, do you?'

He shakes his head.

'And you haven't seen television since this morning?'

'No, I haven't.' Just fucking tell me, he feels like shouting. How can this get any worse?

'I think you better read this.'

He takes the tablet. He is looking at a website. He takes his glasses, cleans them. As he reads the heading – The Confession of Gabriel Roberts – his heart leaps. He starts to devour the words.

I am not, really, Gabriel Roberts, of course.

I wrote "The President" after I was forced to have sex with the CEO of a major international mining company, CanResources. The story wasn't inspired by my encounter with Mr Ivan Capaldi, but it was certainly a response to it. As you may know, CanResources owns gold and platinum mines all over the world. It has been a late starter in Africa, though – and it has been difficult for them to invest in my country, particularly thanks to the onerous legal requirements on new entrants that require them to have a majority stake with the politically correct shade of ownership.

CanResources is, of course, whiter than an Arctic blizzard and so a local partner was found with which they were on the verge of creating a joint venture for its South African operations. On paper, the potential partner was a perfect match – completely Black-owned and run. In reality, though, the choice was causing much consternation among ruling party bigwigs who were outraged CanResources hadn't opted for a company owned by one of their Congress cronies.

Encouraging CanResources to get in bed with the "right" company (the one helmed by the president's nephew, in other words) instead would turn out to be pretty easy. It helped that a senior party member (let's call him by his Struggle-era nomenclature, The Knife) was well aware that – despite Mr Capaldi having a charming blonde wife, three relatively untroubled teenagers and two (according to the *Financial Times*, at any rate) Pekingese – he also had a penchant for young, innocent-looking gentlemen.

That's where I came in. I didn't have to do too much – in fact, all I had to do was show up at Mr Capaldi's hotel suite and be fucked bareback, a cigarette butt burning into my back as he pounded me. The cameras behind the mirrors, the bugs in the lampshades (I assume) – they did the rest.

Now, did I really have to do that? Did I have a choice?

Oh, yeah. Of course I could've said no. But then The Knife would've told my dad that I'm gay. (With the State Security Agency's resources at his disposal, The Knife knows everything – including the more insalubrious reaches of my internet browsing history.)

If The Knife had outed me to my dad, I would've been shunned, disowned, cast out. Bye-bye university. Bye-bye flat. I couldn't face that. I couldn't face the contempt on my dad's face when he told me to fuck off, forever. So what if we have never been close. The scene played over and over in my head – and I still couldn't bear it.

Not long after my encounter with the married magnate from Toronto, I became aware of my father's bid to challenge the constitutionality of the right for people not to be discriminated against on the basis of their sexual orientation. I knew this was a ploy – that it was unlikely this move would make headway; that it was a way of currying favour with traditional leaders and their followers ahead of next year's elections.

It still hurt. It hurt like being fucked in the arse without lube does. (I should know.) I considered my options:

DO NOTHING. Pretend, like I have all my life, that I'm not one of those faggots he despises. Pretend and pray that The Knife doesn't deploy me to provide comforts of a questionable nature to any other visiting FTSE 500 businessmen.

RUN AWAY. But really? As a young, poor university student it's un-likely I would survive (and remain hidden) for very long. Staying alive is an expensive business.

MAKE A STAND. Attempt something that would illuminate the ruling party's hypocrisy – its avarice and cruelty, and the utter contempt it has for decency and the lives of others.

I picked option three. I didn't know whether I would succeed – I often doubted I would. But I tried anyway. I wrote "The President". I submitted it to *Vula*. The editor was gay; the creative director was an ardent feminist and an ally – and so I was pretty certain they would publish it, even if the piece was of dubious literary merit.

I was right – they did publish it. But *Vula* wasn't enough. No one would notice it; it was too small. So I had to resort to legacy media. In life, you are given some measure of luck, I think. And here was mine: my father's fabulous former spokesperson, Connie Msimang, had left his employ, returning to the media in which she has worked for much of her career. She was editing the culture pages at South Africa's sec-ond biggest Sunday paper, and hunting for interesting stories.

I suggested to Connie she should write a feature on *Vula* (it was an easy sell – they're cool young kids doing great stuff blah blah); and then I waited. Here was the biggest risk. I had to tell Connie about *Vula*, but I couldn't let her think I was involved in the publication. I did not want anyone – anyone – to suspect that the author of its most recent story was the son of the Minister of Traditional Affairs; if they did, The Knife would catch wind, and everything would unravel. That's a nice way of saying I'd quickly become "accidental" roadkill.

You're shocked? Trust me, in The Knife's eyes not even the scions of cabinet ministers are above a tactical elimination. It's called "pragmatism". It was a close thing – being the clever (and paranoid) chap that he is, Adam Miller, *Vula*'s editor, quickly smelled a rat. But – and I am immensely grateful for this – he never publicly shared his suspicions about my real identity, not even when everyone was demanding that he reveal who wrote the story.

The other risk was that Connie would just forget about my suggestion. "The President" would quickly sink into inconsequence if she did that. But – thankfully – she didn't. She interviewed them (thank you, Connie!).

And then the world went mad. Oh, the fury! The wounded pride! How dare someone imagine that our beloved president (God bless his four wives) is QUEER!

They were all dying to know who wrote it, so they could show him a thing or two. Some cheeky whitey, they thought.

I have thought about the future and have decided I don't have one – at least not one I actually want to live. I was born in Maputo. After my mother was murdered by the apartheid police, I spent my early years in London. Neither Mozambique nor England are home. And South Africa, which I have lived in since I was 14? That is my father's country; it is not my own. The more I've mulled it over, the more I can't possibly imagine feeling truly at home in a place where you can't express yourself freely, and where you can't be who you are. And so, *adieu*.

"The President" was undoubtedly revenge: against my father, against the hypocrisy, the greed and the expediency of his party and comrades. But it isn't revenge simply for its own sake. Because, in the aftermath of this, I hope my father will reconsider his intolerance. I hope that one day my country's much-vaunted liberation becomes more than just a word – that people really are able to write what they like, and love whoever they want to, without fear of censure from government or society.

If anything, the reaction to "The President" has shown we are some way off reaching that.

Suraya, thank you for being there. Adam, I'm sorry. I love you.

That's it now. I'm signing off now.

This is the end.

Epilogue

It is not the end.

The world turns. The days gather. The words are written. For those of us left behind, it is not the end.

And, here I am, driving over the mountains, spurred on by the cicadas' thrum, splashing through the mirages dancing on the tar. The road twists; the scrubby green folds rise and fall around me, occasionally revealing the Atlantic's blue curves.

I wonder if Max might have imagined this – what did he see when he looked down from that balustrade; what future did he foretell?

Perhaps he didn't care. Perhaps he didn't care what would happen to all of us, what would happen next. I doubt that, though. He wanted to change things, even just a little. And he did – he did something, and sometimes something is enough. Now it is up to us. The completed manuscript is in the fat manila envelope on the seat next to me. My stomach quivers. Will Adam sit down to read it as soon as I give it to him? Will he like it? Does it matter whether he does, or does not? After all: I didn't write it for him, anyway – I wrote it for me; I wrote it for Max.

I'm headed to Adam now with the manuscript, yes. But we're jumping ahead. While I'm driving, let me take you back to the beginning – the beginning after the end. The TV bulletins, the radio reports, the headlines on papers and websites all screaming the same thing: Max is dead.

Suraya, thank you for being there.

That's all he said. A thank-you. I didn't want it. It couldn't fill this new emptiness. It couldn't make up for Max disappearing like that, no warning, no hug goodbye.

It didn't feel real, reading his confession. It didn't feel real, reading that thank-you.

Because I had hardly been there – an extra while the great drama unfolded off-stage, in his dark. It stings: I am embarrassed I didn't notice more. I was Woolf-stoned, lost in Joyce. Agonizing over a disappointing mark, dreading the imminence of another essay due, dazzled – or disappointed – by all the books I'd been reading.

What had I known?

Nothing, really. He had told me his mother had died when he was very young; but he never talked about her. His dad – he had once said he was in business; he did not say what kind of business. I had no idea he was a cabinet minister's son. And can you blame me? He used his mother's maiden name instead of his father's surname! Yes: he put 'Smythe' on his assignments. And, in this epoch, Smythes do not run government departments, as a rule – certainly not ones overseeing 'traditional affairs'.

I had known nothing; I had done nothing. Now he was dead. Now I wanted to get to know him. I wanted to understand. It wouldn't bring him back – duh – but it would be something. It wouldn't make amends. But, if I was going to let go, I needed to know what I was letting go of. I needed fiction to make Max real. And so that is why, after I had dabbed away the tears, switched off the TV and shut down my computer, I decided to find Adam. Easier said than done. The website of the branding agency he and Zandile owned was down; the emails to an address I'd managed to find after hours of Googling were bouncing back. I did not give up. I found his surname in the telephone directory. There was no Miller, A. in it. Of course there wasn't; what 28-year-old has a landline?!

'Oh, he was at Rondebosch Boys a couple grades below me,' said my brother when I told him over drinks.

'You were at school with Adam Miller?' I asked, shocked.

'Yep, thought you knew that. We were both library monitors. Nice guy. He lived in Newlands, I think.'

Back to the phone directory. I found just one Miller entry listed with a street address in Newlands. I drove there. A woman answered after I'd rung the doorbell for a third time. I said: 'I need to find Adam – Adam Miller – please.'

'I don't know who that is,' she said crisply.

Before she could walk away from the intercom, I said, in a rush, 'Please. I beg you. I'm the best friend of the guy who wrote the story that Adam published. I have to find him – Adam. I have to talk to him. Please. Tell me where he is?'

The gate buzzed in reply. I pushed it open and marched up the stepping stones to the rose-fringed front door. A middle-aged woman had opened the door, was standing behind the still-closed security gate.

'I'm not sure I should be doing this,' she told me, biting her lip. 'I don't think he wants to see anyone. I think he just wants to be left alone.'

I nodded daintily. 'Of course, I understand. It's been a terrible shock.'
I didn't have to act: the weeping that began then was real, completely real.

'Sorry,' I whispered. 'I'm so sorry. I... just... really... wanted... to... talk to...
him.'

She sighed. I could see though my tears that she was still doubtful of
whether she was doing the right thing. But she straightened up and said,
finally, 'He's gone to his aunt's place in Kommetjie. But please, *please* don't
tell anyone else he's there.'

And so I drove this very road, Ou Kaapse Weg. I wasn't sad – I was angry,
I realised. Max never told me anything. He had thought I couldn't be trusted.
It hurt. If only he had said something. Then the anger faded – because what
could I have done then? Even had I known, what could I honestly have done?
There was only now. That's why I was driving.

The city was forgotten, and now the mountains surrendered to the sea.
The road continued, past marshland and vlei, then up again, etched into cliff-
side. A sprinkling of houses appeared above a blazing strand.

I double-checked the address, rang the bell. Adam came out of his aunt's
clapboard cottage, walked up to the gate, hesitant and fretful. He looked
different to the pictures I had seen of him in the papers – weary, older, his
hair ruffed up.

'Sorry to disturb.' I explained to him who I was. I told him that his stepmom had told me where he was. I told him that I wanted to – I needed to – talk.

'Is your phone on?'

'Yes. Why?'

'Switch it off and take the battery out. I don't want them knowing where
I am if I can help it. They've probably already figured it out, though. Zandile
had left hers on when she came to say goodbye.' He looked glum.

'The government?'

'Yes, the government. They can tell where you are by tracking the location
of your cellphone.'

I switched the phone off. Didn't tell him it was doubtful the government
would be spying on little me. He invited me inside, with obvious reluctance.
He did not want me here. He had come here to be alone, but he was too
polite to say so. We had tea, out on the deck. At first we didn't talk: we just
held our mugs, watching the ocean's smash and shimmer. The sun was soft;
it felt like spring was seeping in from over the scrubby hills behind us.

We did not talk, and then we did – or he did – until it got too cold, until he lit a fire for us in the living room's fireplace. We drank two bottles of wine that night, and the words continued, sloppier and thicker now, sometimes with tears. Adam didn't mind that my voice recorder was running. He didn't mind when I told him to pause while I quickly inserted fresh AAA batteries.

I did not think too much, did not feel too much – just listened and scribbled down notes.

'I'm going to write a story,' I finally told him. 'I'm going to write what happened. Exactly what happened. Or as close to it as I can manage.'

I didn't at first. I couldn't. The words were hidden – they were somewhere, but out of reach. In the weeks that followed, I tried to forget. I watched movies. I made koesisters with my *ouma* (who was kind enough not to ask why I wasn't on campus).

Even while I was away from university, Max refused to disappear. I kept the radio off; I did not read the newspapers. But somehow it leaked in anyway – I knew what they were saying. I heard about the press conference, the minister's mournful statement about his troubled son who had lost the battle with mental illness. Paranoid schizophrenia. He spoke of the 'tragic delusions' that drove his sweet, sensitive son to an untimely, unnecessary end. Minister Lindela was very convincing – especially when he choked up, told the world he had failed his son. 'I wasn't there for him when he needed me most,' he said, between sobs.

It worked, mostly – the tabloids fell for it. Minister's "crazy" son said one headline. MAD MAX! screeched another.

Clever, so clever. Had The Knife thought this up? Razor sharp, that one – and impregnable as steel. There was no resignation, nothing. Just a weeping minister misremembering his son. Of course Adam released a statement. He told the world: the minister is a liar. Max was not mad.

New Era published excerpts of leaked medical records from a military hospital. A diagnosis for Max Smythe: schizophrenic. Other papers, ones whose owners weren't quite so pally with the president, asked the psychiatrist whose name was on the records for comment. And those papers, the *Daily Times* among them, studiously informed their readers that the psychiatrist refused to comment, refused to confirm whether or not the records were genuine. But he didn't have to – there was the evidence, his evidence: schizophrenic. The papers quoted Adam again, ranting – 'They're fake! The diagnosis is doctored! They're from a military hospital for God's sake. How can you trust them?'

So very clever. Just as clever as Mr Ivan Capaldi's prerecorded announcement that – although he had met many wonderful people on his trip to South Africa – Minister Lindela's son was not one of them. The denial had been filmed with Capaldi's marionette wife smiling supportively next to him. There was no sign of the Pekingese. Again: no resignation. *Niks*, nada, *fokol*.

But what if it wasn't clever? What if it was just true? What if Max had imagined all of this? Then I remembered Dr Khumalo. I went to her.

'You were Max Smythe's doctor,' I said once I had sat down in her consultation room. 'We were best friends – I brought him here once when he had flu. You have to tell me. Did he ever see you about...'

I petered out, unable to finish the sentence. She looked at me, inscrutable, waiting.

I took a breath, tried again. 'I think his dad's lying. I think Max was telling the truth. I think Max was forced to have sex with that horrible Canadian man. Did he ever come to you about this?'

'Suraya...'

I lost it. 'He's fucking dead. I want to get to the bottom of this. I want the truth. Just, please, tell me.'

And so she told me. She told me that she wouldn't know whether or not Max had been schizophrenic – they hadn't done the tests for that; she was a GP, not a psychiatrist. This is what she knew, though: when he came to her, he was certainly anxious – extremely anxious. He was clearly scared he had been infected with something. He had had sex, unprotected sex with someone. If he had been telling the truth, his worry seemed reasonable, not paranoid. There was nothing more that she knew. She had tried to get him to talk about it, but he'd stayed tight-lipped.

I thanked her. I asked her not to tell anyone I had come to see her. I went for a walk in Newlands Forest afterwards. I looked left, expecting him to be there, but of course he wasn't; there were just the pines and shadows and shards of light. I heard a scream, or perhaps it was crow's cry, snatched in the breeze, or nothing, nothing at all. I carried on walking until the trees relented, stopped to stare down at the city. I sat on the bench we used to sit on. I did not want to count the days; they were too heavy; they were too much.

At home I began listening to the recordings I'd made with Adam. I listened through the night. I slept in the morning, getting up again at noon. I listened to them again. My notebook was a mess of lines and words and numbers. I made myself Earl Grey. And then I sat down at my laptop. The cursor flashed.

And then I wrote the beginning. I wrote: Is this how the story ends?

How will the story end?

I did not think about that in the weeks that followed. I wrote. I attended university again – properly, like I used to, like I used to when I enjoyed it. But the best times, the bearable times, were when I was in my flat, at my laptop. Even if I was just staring at the words, waiting for more. He was in the words; the words made him, they made him real again even if they did not bring him back.

I stopped missing him. I was with him. I dreaded sleep. That's when he'd disappear. I'd dream about The Knife – he would jump out of the darkness, with blades instead of digits, like a monster in a Scooby-Doo flick. I would run and run and run and as the tips of steel sliced my back I would wake up.

I wanted to call Adam, but I thought it better, safer not to. I still kept tabs on him, though. With Zandile now overseas, there was no more *Vula*, no more branding agency. Instead, a new magazine: *Bamukele*. Embrace. A magazine for LGBT voices; for online-only for now, but with plans for a quarterly print edition. Funded by an American NGO, and various Scandinavian embassies. (As yet, none of the stories published have featured a gay president.)

Yes: I wanted to call Adam, wanted to talk with him, but I wasn't prepared to risk it. Rather just write, I told myself. Write like your life – and his – depended on it. Keep writing, and soon enough, *The President* would be ready, and the next chapter could begin.

From my early teens, I was an avid reader of the columns in *Business Day* authored by the human rights activist Rhoda Kadalie. Her writings gave the impression of an author who was outspoken, principled and incorruptible: someone not seduced by the trappings of power and money – instead offering a clear-eyed, strident critique of those who were. In my second-last year of school, her daughter, Julia, introduced me to her mother. Rhoda, in time, became a friend, a mentor and a confidant – someone who I could be my whole self in front of, who loved me unconditionally. Every so often, Rhoda would take me out for lunch, regaling me with gossip, anecdotes and analysis. I absolutely adored her.

When *In Your Face*, a collection of her columns, was published in 2009, Rhoda scrawled in the front of my copy: "With much admiration for the enfant terrible of the 21st Century". Back then, I suppose I was actually something akin to that. I wrote outraged blog posts and letters to newspaper editors, typically decrying corruption, injustice and predation (often the same, or similar, territory to what Rhoda wrote about in her columns). Rhoda encouraged these outpourings. She had an instinctive dislike for hierarchy, hypocrisy, venality and out-of-touch elites. She was both a role model, and a cheerleader. She believed my voice mattered, and that I shouldn't be shy about using it. I'm so grateful for her encouragement.

While our respective political views increasingly diverged in the last few years of her life, we both shared an unstinting belief in vigorous accountability and critique – in the importance of speaking truth to power. We never spoke about the biblical story of David and his triumph over Goliath, but I strongly believe both of us would have been rooting for David (regardless of our differing views on President Trump!).

The last time I saw Rhoda was in 2019, when we watched the LA Philharmonic perform at the Hollywood Bowl (by then she lived in California, and I would soon end up living there too). She passed away in 2022 after a short battle with lung cancer. There are moments when I still find it impossible that someone so lively and wonderful is no longer here, and moments when her absence fills me with an inconsolable aching. In a small way, this novel seeks to live up to Rhoda's feisty, irreverent example. Rest in peace, my beloved friend.

The President is a work of fiction. It is, however, chiefly inspired by the political backlash to a painting by Brett Murray, *The Spear*, in 2012. It draws on interviews I conducted with the artist as well as news coverage and opinion pieces from the time. One front page headline in particular sticks out: a pastor calling for Brett to be stoned. The threats made by ANC bigwigs, their attempts to stymie creative expression and free speech – all that shook my faith in South Africa as a constitutional democracy, and in the ANC's commitment to the human rights enshrined in a constitution that the party had, itself, been instrumental in drafting.

I wrote the first drafts of the novel in 2013 and 2014 as an attempt to grapple with these feelings, to reflect on the ANC's seemingly autocratic and intolerant turn. I sought to gain a better understanding of how and why backlash happens – and the way a response to art can be manipulated, exploited and inflamed to further specific political ends.

Brett patiently and graciously fielded my impertinent questions about what it was like to have invoked the fury of a power-drunk governing party (this included tapped phones, legal action and threats so vituperative his family went into hiding). Thank you, Brett. Another Brett (also an accomplished artist) – Brett Seiler – generously shared his reflections on queer life in Zimbabwe, a country which has experienced a far more significant lurch into autocracy than South Africa has (or, I suspect, is ever likely to). The account of life under fatwa in *Joseph Anton*, Salman Rushdie's memoir, also offered helpful context. *External Mission* by Stephen Ellis, *Askari* by Jacob Dlamini, and the podcast, *They Killed Dulcie*, helped me better understand the ANC in exile during apartheid.

I extend grateful thanks to my dear friend and writing buddy, Erin Conway-Smith, for her extremely helpful feedback on various iterations of the manuscript.

Thank you to Penny Kew, whose high school English classes were both liberating and possibly life-saving. Thank you Bettina Stiemeder, Andrea Nattrass, Fourie Botha and Damon Galgut. Without Amelia

Greenhall's inspirational writings on what it means to be an artist publisher, I might never have mustered the wherewithal to wrestle this book into print. Thank you, Christian, for your close reads of the new draft, and for your enthusiastic, loving support. Thank you, Catarina, for the striking book design and for the many years of collaborating. May there be many more!

It is dismaying that the themes *The President* is preoccupied with seem to loom as large now as they did when I was working on the original manuscript over a decade ago. In far too many countries, populist demagoguery has flourished and minorities are scapegoated for all manner of ills. As I write this, Donald Trump's second presidential administration has launched a multi-pronged attack on LGBT rights, with vicious ire directed at America's trans people in particular. The president's callous bigotry extends far beyond the US with a funding freeze that has led to sudden and lasting disruptions to healthcare for queer people and other marginalized groups in South Africa and elsewhere.

Jacob Zuma, South Africa's own populist, homophobic kleptocrat – who had for many years seemed Teflon-resistant to scandal – resigned in 2018. In 2006, long before his fall from grace, Zuma described gay marriage as 'a disgrace to the nation and to God'. In 2024, at a rally for his breakaway party, uMkhonto Wesizwe (MK), he once again described gay marriage as 'a disgrace'. He promised that an MK election victory would lead to the repeal of gay marriage legislation, and called for there to be 'African law' rather than 'Dutch law'. These chilling echoes of the rhetoric found in *The President* to justify an erosion of LGBT rights offer a warning to not take South Africa's progressive constitution (and provisions like same-sex marriage which flow from it) for granted. It's not merely a matter of the law. Hate crimes against LGBT people continue. In January 2025, the world's first openly gay imam was murdered near the South African city of Gqeberha in what appears to have been an assassination.

Now in his early 80s, Mr Zuma plays a much more marginal but still ominous role, wielding false promises, outrage and charisma with sufficient deftness that MK did well enough at the most recent elections to help deprive his erstwhile political home, the ruling African National Congress, of its majority.

It would be folly to assume that demagogues like Zuma are guaranteed to be in South Africa's political wilderness forever. The comeback of Trump – his return to power some four years after inciting an attempted insurrection – offers a chilling reminder. So does Brexit, and the resurgence of far-right parties in Europe. A reminder, yes, that extremist, bigoted populism finds fertile ground where there is grievance, alienation and dissatisfaction. The longer South Africa remains afflicted by steep inequalities and persistent poverty, the more vulnerable it is to demagoguery's return.

COLOPHON

TITLE

The President

EDITION

First paperback edition, 2025

PUBLISHER

PRONK
An imprint of Pronk Press
Ukiah, California ~ Cape Town, South Africa
pronk.press

ORIGINAL DESIGN

Voodoo Voodoo studio
Catarina Pereira
voodoovoodoo.net

PAPERBACK EDITION LAYOUT

Pulp Paperworks
Johannesburg, South Africa

ISBN: 978-1-967449-03-3
Library of Congress Control Number: 2025916565